I0587065

PLAY OF SHADOWS

PLAY OF SHADOWS

KATHRYN PURNELL

J R Garran

Title: Play of Shadows – Indonesian Short Stories

Author: Kathryn Purnell (1911-2006)

First published in 2022

Copyright © J R Garran

ISBN 978-0-6488606-4-8

Ebook ISBN 978-0-6488606-3-1

A catalogue entry for this book is available from The National Library of Australia
www.trove.nla.gov.au

Editor's Note: These short stories were written in the 1950s during the author's time in Jakarta as the wife of a United Nations diplomat . Some of the language and opinions expressed may seem old-fashioned or even offensive to certain readers. For the sake of authenticity it was decided to allow the stories to reflect the time during which they were written.

Contents

BRIDGE
NEIGHBOURS

In retrospect, my experience of Indonesia – both philosophical and enigmatical – owed much to the view from our small balcony, built as an upstairs decoration by some Dutch official long since disinherited. It was not just that it provided the quiet consolation of resting the eyes on water. It was also a guardhouse post with both the advantages and drawbacks of a box at the opera, where it was possible to observe with impersonal pleasure and personal apprehension the natural temper of the bridge population. I was constrained to sit and think on that balcony. Its capacity was four rattan chairs with room for feet, off or on the railing. A cool drink was reached from the floor without the effort of shifting weight and the head relaxed against the wall, supported through necessity at exactly the right angle for maximum visual participation. Always the scene was panoramic, from the clouds that raced across the blue sky and shadowed the slope of green grass above the sun-shimmered river; to the bridge over which the varied traffic trotted, wheeled or drove, and under which my bridge neighbours lived. It is possible that the man who invented Cinerama was once stranded on a similar balcony in Jakarta.

Our house was at the point where the river turned, and on the far side of the bridge the street we faced became the main road to the mountains. It was easy to see from the balcony that a bridge is a splendid shelter from sun and rain when a river provides fresh water. A home, after all, is basically a shelter with water. Food, the other requirement for maintaining life, is always precarious anyway, dependant as it is on day-to-day intake. Security may seem to you and me the means to provide money to buy the necessities and extravagances we need and want. I found it enlightening to watch the bridge people who considered security to be shelter and water, on the assumption that if they did not eat they would die anyway. The struggle for food was fundamental for straight-out survival, a case of you push and I go down, or I push and you go down – as simple as that. I realised with new perception as I watched from my balcony that food merely meant the day-to-day acceptance of hours of grinding toil, but that fresh running water was, by its very nature, the gift of God – and shelter by a river the first balance of aesthetic comfort. Since the beginning of time it has been worth man's while to fight for a shelter near a river. On behalf of my bridge neighbours in Jakarta, this security battle was waged by four old women.

Now, Jakarta is a large city of well over three million people and urban society in our times requires strict laws to protect the combined body of the whole against the individual peculiarities of separate citizens. It was, of course, against the law to take up residence under a bridge that crossed the river as it flowed through the city. It was particularly forbidden in a part of the city where the bridge linked the university and the homes of the wealthy on the road that led to the famous botanical gardens, the country palace of the President, and beyond that the cool air of the mountains.

The bridge people were, therefore, very conscious of the delicate situation surrounding their tenancy of our section of the river. Not, mind you, that other than catastrophe would move them, for they assumed correctly that if they accepted the threat of a police blitz at face value and departed temporarily, replacements would be well-established before their return. The police were not unaware of the truth of this assumption and did their rounds with gracious acceptance of the small gratuities offered by the otherwise homeless for the privilege of obeying the rules of squatting at a good address.

The area around the bridge was, except for our premises, an open terrain of green grass between the road and the river. It was some time before I realised that a new, foreign occupation of our upstairs flat constituted the gravest possible hazard to the bridge people. We overlooked the river, the opposite expanse of grassy slope, and the four corner apartments under the bridge. The enforcement of the law and, in consequence, the squeeze, depended on the measure of our tolerance or its opposite – the virulence of our complaints.

After our arrival, the first manoeuvre of the bridge people was to pretend they were casual visitors making use of the river as a free public bath. During my first weeks of odd moments on the balcony, I was charmed to see beautiful girls walk down the slopes, spread a sarong on the riverbank, slip into the water fully clothed, remove the sarong they were wearing under the water, wash it with soap and throw it up on the grass. After this, they would swim a little, bob up and down in the water like mermaids with tails well hidden, long hair floating and breasts semi-obscured in the splash. The intriguing moment of thwarted suspense would come when they stepped like nymphs out of the river and into the waiting sarong like a flash in the sunlight. I was always reminded of the trout that got away. The washed sarong was then spread out to dry and the girl, or girls as the case might be, sat down beside it to comb and dress her hair.

It was only after my household was settled that I had time to stay long enough on the balcony to recognise the repetitive colour patterns of the cotton sarongs. Then, one morning, a girl appeared from under the corner of the bridge across the river in my direct line of vision, stretched her arms above her head, looked up toward our balcony, stooped, and disappeared under the bridge again. Five minutes later the same girl walked nonchalantly down the slope from the road to take her bath.

The section of the river slope that I could see from the balcony was kept scrupulously clean. This was a constant source of amazement to me, because after nightfall the sound of activity across the river was of a dimension that left no doubt that the area was as busy as a public park. Food vendors called their wares and the spicy aroma of fried rice floated into our garden. Voices called, and sometimes I heard the beat of a drum and often the plaintive wail of a bamboo flute. There were evening swimming parties, and shadows danced in the light of tiny fires. A line of betjaks was always parked near the bridge and children ran about at the edge of the road. Yet by eight o'clock in the morning, only a green and silver silence surrounded the river until the girls came to bathe and the odd hot traveller put down his baskets to cool himself. There was no litter; even the ashes of the riverbank fires had been swept away into the fast flow of the water.

It was a month before I even saw the grandmothers. It was inevitable, I suppose, that I should first make the acquaintance of Grandmother One, for she was in charge of the apartment under the corner of the bridge directly beneath the high hedge of our garden. I could not see from the balcony the narrow and inconvenient portion of riverbank she kept tidy in case of my prying eyes. I discovered her first when I stood with Punip, in his capacity as gardener, persuading him that it was better not to trim the hibiscus shrubs that so successfully screened our triangle corner from the traffic on the bridge. I heard a child wail on the other side of the hedge and, with a natural curiosity I find hard to restrain, looked over from a precarious perch on the wheelbarrow. When my face appeared, Grandmother One put the baby down and stood herself respectfully up in consternation and alarm. I smiled for I was equally surprised and what else could I do? Grandmother One forced a toothless grin in return, gathering up her paraphernalia – including the baby – and shot like a rabbit under the bridge.

Three or four mornings later, having suffered a hot and wakeful night, I decided to try the balcony for a river breeze. Already, the traffic was thick on the road and not a betjak was parked by the bridge. Grandmother Two was busy on the opposite bank, picking up papers, skins and packets, which she held close to her eyes long enough to decide which of her two rattan baskets was worthy to receive the offerings. Her choice was obviously tantalising and her eyesight poor, for the process was slow and one of the baskets, much larger than the other, was already full. As I watched, she walked to the riverbank and, with a gesture of distaste, unceremoniously dumped the contents of the largest basket into the river. She had worked her way practically back to the bridge when she suddenly straightened a little and waved a bony arm to someone further along whom I could not see but suspected was Grandmother Three busily engaged in some occupation. Sure enough, this much more agile grandmother appeared with two small children in tow, one lugging a large empty basket and the other, barely able to walk, clutching her hand. The two old ladies sat down momentarily on the grass and compared the contents of the small baskets. Then they rose and disappeared into the twilight under the bridge.

If you walked straight out our front driveway and crossed the main road, you could follow a wide dirt and gravel path along the river for half a kilometre. The riverbank was steep here under some ancient willows, and the path petered out in a shaggy banana grove where another street finished at the river. This area was the playground of the river children and the domain of Grandmother Four, who made sure none of them swam further down where respectable citizens such as those who lived and worked in our street might see and report them. On this side of the bridge, Grandmother Four safely spread her washing in the midday sun and ran a few chickens as well. Grandmother One, living right under our hedge, was less fortunate and had to use discretion in respect to both washing and the baby left in her charge from dawn until dusk. So every afternoon she took the baby in her arms to sit in safety besides Grandmother Four, and very often Grandmothers Two and Three, across the road under a gnarled old willow so close to the river that its shelter provided a hide with an excellent lookout under both sides of the bridge and around the banks past our house.

One early afternoon after a morning of torrential rain, I happened to look out of my front window and saw the four grandmothers assembling under this tree. Grandmother Four had spread a mat on the mud and, with Grandmother One, waited for the arrival of the other two by foot across the bridge. The sun had come out and pale blue wisps of steam rose like shadows above the silvery water and shaded to mauve the pink hibiscus flowers along my front fence. It was the hour when most of labouring Jakarta lay down where they happened to be and slept. After the grandmothers put the infants to sleep in a row on another mat, they bowed to each and sat down, for all the world like my childish imaginings of the witches of Macbeth. It was too much for me. I put on my shoes and went for a stroll along the river, full of curiosity to see closely the faces of the old ones who guarded precincts of the bridge. My sudden appearance startled the grandmothers, who were sitting in a semi-circle facing back towards the darker depths of water under the span. They were all ancient crones with thin, carved cheek bones prominent above toothless mouths. Four pairs of sharp black piercing eyes glanced with undisguised hostility at my face. I stopped, bent over the babies, put my finger to my lips and smiled at Grandmother One who was, of course, the only one I had seen close enough to recognise. But even she did not respond, so I walked on. The sweet perfume of showered frangipani mingled in the air with the dark-brown smell of sodden earth. The river shone iridescent as the sunlight sparkled in the rising drifts of steam. I thought how I would like to sit under the last willow where the banana grove led away from the river at right angles down the street that paralleled my own. I felt ostracised by the unfriendly old women and resentful of the fear of my predecessors that caused it.

The little houses on the parallel street were innocently unpretentious and the gardens delightfully shaggy, without the barrier of high hedges, so the walk around the block was pleasant under the clean trees smelling of spice and honey. By the time I walked back through my own gate I felt unexpectedly satisfied and decided that I would go again in the quiet hour of another afternoon when the sun came out after the rain. It was perhaps ten days later such opportunity came, but only three ancient ones preferred not to see me and looked down when I passed. Grandmother One was no longer invited to watch from the shade of the willow. Nor did the others wave to her across the water in the early hours of morning. As far as her colleagues were concerned, she could keep the baby she minded quietly under her own corner of the bridge and suffer the consequence of her indiscretion. This was resented as my fault, although I did not realise it.

The day before had been one of the socially busy days when my husband was in Singapore and I was trying to use discretion in my demands for the official car during office hours. Traffic being what it is in Jakarta, driving myself and the use of the betjak constituted a risk I could not take without upsetting conjugal equilibrium. I was not, by any means, the only wife who suffered such restraint, so we circumvented the problem with an intricate pick-up and drop-off system that placed no noticeable strain on anyone's official car and depended not a little on brave American women who stuck to the assumption that they drove as well as their husbands. On this occasion I had set out for luncheon in our car, picked up an English friend who also needed transport, and after our arrival, dismissed the driver on office business. I returned as one of four in the car of an American lady at three o'clock in the afternoon. My car was in the driveway, parked in readiness to take me out again at five. The office staff had gone home and the silence of heavy heat lay on the garden as recumbent as my houseboy and the driver who rested on the grass out of sight in the shade of the sugar-palm and my balcony. At least, I presumed they were there since my footsteps above generally aroused Punip from this spot on other afternoons.

We caught Grandmother One red-handed hanging out her washing on my front fence. It was just too bad; my car was obviously waiting to take me out; there was no sign of the driver or anyone else keeping busy – which usually indicated I was resting; no visitors ever called before four o'clock; the tuan was away. It was miserably bad look that I should suddenly return with three foreign ladies who had accepted my invitation for a quick cold drink. It was quite evident that all these ladies were shocked and indignant on my behalf. Grandmother One clearly wished the river would swallow her up in the sure knowledge that her days under the bridge were numbered. She tried to bow as if she belonged and gathered up the wet washing while we went past her through the gate. It was the wrong kind of washing and the three grandmothers who stood up under the willow tree across the road knew it. Altogether we were eight women and we knew it.

"What a cheek!" my American friend said, "I suppose she's the babu of some of the boys who work in the office."

"No," I replied, and could have bitten out my tongue. "She lives under the bridge."

"It's revolting," the English friend decided.

"It is against the law, but as fast as the police move squatters out, they move back again. You will be all right, though. You can lodge an official complaint through the office and have them cleared out. The government doesn't want them there. You know how it is − nothing is ever done until you made a fuss."

"Well," I countered, "I suppose if they are pushed out, they have nowhere else to go."

The Dutch friend sighed and took pity on my ignorance.

"You cannot risk having such camper near," she told me. "It is not safe. You might feel sorry for an old babu but she is probably looking after girls. You may not have noticed the girls because they only come out at night. You can guess what they are and the types they bring around, from betjak-drivers and pedlars to thieves and guerrillas from the hills. First one old woman moves in like that, and before long you have no idea who is there and what they might do. You must report them for your own safety, indeed you must."

As I'd expected, Punip heard our feet and turned up in his white coat to serve the drinks. My Dutch friend took the opportunity to speak to him in Bahasa and then waited diplomatically until he had departed to speak to me again.

"I asked him about the babu," she informed me, "and his answer was just what I expected. I imagine he has been either bribed or frightened, probably both. He would only say the old grandmother was harmless and better than the last lot that lived under the corner of the bridge."

I thanked her for her concern and changed the subject. I think she thought I took the dangers of living in Jakarta lightly, which I did not. After the ladies went on their way, I dismissed Punip and made myself another drink to take to the balcony. The smoke of my cigarette curled into a question-mark above the river. Although my recent visitors did not know it, I had to multiply one harmless old grandmother by four and admit to myself that I had not only seen and admired the beauty of the girls but noticed the constant row of betjaks. Yet somehow, I could not see the problem as a matter of immediate personal safety to be solved by police action that might temporarily clear the people from under the bridge. I tended to see it rather as a question of "the devil you know and the devil you don't". Since there were, at that time, over three million people living in Jakarta, a city planned to absorb half a million, it was inevitable that dry empty space, no matter how precarious in the eyes of the law, would always be occupied – if not by per-manent, then by casual tenancies. Also, I had to concede that bridges, even in normally populated Western cities and towns, had attracted a certain kind of evening occupation since time immemorial. From the practical point of view, if "this lot" were, as Punip said, better than the "last lot", what guarantee would I have of the "next lot"? It seemed to me the four watchdog grandmothers had the bridge people well under control; they looked after the babies and the manners of the children and were also very clean. I decided to overlook the matter of the washing and continue to observe the interesting phenomena of the grandmothers.

It took all of three weeks for Grandmother One to regain her status under the willow tree. By that time, it was obvious I had refrained from calling the police and given her another chance. Under these circumstances, the other grandmothers felt they could afford to do likewise and I found myself grateful to them. To see the representatives of all four corners sitting to-gether gave a sense of solidarity to the relationship of "this lot" in their capacity of being better than "the last lot". I made occasion to take a third walk after still another rainy morning, and this time was greeted by respectful toothless smiles all round. Indeed, I turned out to be a friendly, soft and juicy victim of witches' wisdom, quite unaware that Grandmother One was paying tribute for the privilege of reinstatement in the form of my large and luscious paw-paws as they ripened on the trees.

Perhaps I should explain about the paw-paws. They ripened several at a time, with the help of a brown paper bag tied on at the exact moment when their plump green showed signs of turning yellow. The paw-paw is a long, thin, palm-like single stem that rises like a rocket to a height of seven or eight feet in as many months and immediately produces fruit. Every morning the ripe ones were taken down by Punip, who also bagged the next inline for ripening. Always, the house cook Sura received a beautiful specimen for my daily fruit salad but the fate of the remaining ripe ones that were picked at the same time was a mystery I suspected could be easily solved at the hour of my servant's return to the kampong. Only once had I demanded two paw-paws because of guests for dinner, and the ensuing consternation had provided the kitchen with a new system that held an extra in reserve in case I asked again. We had a row of nine paw-paw trees down one side of the driveway, and four or five brown paper bags were in evidence every day, to be tactfully ignored as long as my needs were met. The disappearance of three bags nightly was, therefore, a delicate matter that was not brought to my attention until the inevitable time when only three bags holding a ripe paw-paw were waiting to be plucked.

At first, it was hopefully put to me that paw-paw production had slowed to zero. Unfortunately, I had noticed the three bags the evening before, as well as the usual number of green fruit. It had to be admitted the paw-paws had been stolen and not for the first time. In fact, the thieving had been investigated and pointed as straight as an arrow to the old woman across the road, for that one had offered a paw-paw for sale the day before yesterday and where would she get a paw-paw? My answer to this question was dampening, for I could see no reason why she could not have bought herself a paw-paw to sell or received one as a gift. She had never sold one before, to Punip's knowledge, and according to his inquiries yesterday, she never left the river. She was a sly one, he informed me knowingly, not like the grandmother under our corner of the bridge who looked after the baby. Inwardly I was inclined to agree with him, but I made it outwardly plain that I didn't think it right to accuse anybody of stealing three paw-paw daily for who knows how long on the strength of one paw-paw offered for sale the day before yesterday.

Punip said he would mount guard himself that very night and catch the culprit. He caught Grandmother One with a long bamboo pole with a wire on the end of it, which landed the paw-paws right into her cleaning basket.

There was no doubt that Punip was chagrined to have to tell me about Grandmother One, who had been terrified when he caught her and wept for his forgiveness. She had not done it for herself but only to keep the peace under the bridge, for her neighbours said that if the nonja had been so kind as to excuse her for the washing, she would also overlook the theft of one ripe paw-paw each that she could well spare from her foreign abundance. She had not stolen a paw-paw for herself and would never steal from the nonja who had not sent her away with her granddaughter's baby to live on the street. Punip looked at me hard when he told me this and shook his head. He had allowed her to go back to the baby under the bridge, he said, and she was waiting there now. What was I going to do?

I did not have the faintest idea what to do. I felt like a hunter with a gun in his hand who did not know where the trigger was. I told Punip I would let him know later and, in the meantime, to please put all the paw-paws on the bench in the kitchen. "All?" he repeated. "Yes, all," I snapped. Then I took myself to the balcony and stared at the river. There was not a soul on the grassy bank, not one beautiful girl splashing beside her sunlit sarong, not a paper, not a box. Great water-logged clouds were pushing the heat haze from the horizon. The atmosphere was close and sticky. Soon it would rain. My dress was like a plaster on my back and my hair stuck limply to my forehead. The heat sucked the substance of my thought beyond concentration. Somewhere down below near the bridge a baby cried and was immediately hushed. It was, of course, my baby; just as the grandmothers were my grandmothers, even though it was apparent they had to be taught a lesson.

The four grandmothers did not take their places under the willow that afternoon. More ominous still, not one put out washing. The river still flowed under a misty weight of oppressive heat. I wondered, as I stared out my front window, if a witch's pot of cock's blood, mice tails and bat's fur was stirring under the dark recesses of the bridge. Certainly a feeling of guilt had come from somewhere to sit on my shoulders. Punip and Sura had not gone home to the kampong but were sitting sleepily on the back step, waiting. Punip had made a point of reminding me, when I rose from the lunch table, that Grandmother One was still miserably ensconced in the same place on the other side of our hedge. There was no use pretending that I did not know that it would be Grandmother One who would suffer the result of the witch's brew, and who would look after the baby then? Perhaps, I pondered wearily, Punip and Sura were frightened that if I did not show the initiative expected of me, an evening collection would be taken up under the bridge to buy the services of a real sorcerer to settle the matter.

On an impulse I walked to the balcony and was surprised to see the barely distinguishable shadow of Grandmothers Two and Three sitting under the bridge staring with what could

scarcely be other than sympathy in the direction of Grandmother One across the river.

This could only mean one thing. Grandmother Four was the
leader; the toll-collector, as Punip suggested – the sly one. I
had hoped for a rest. Instead, I put a dress over my petticoat
and shoes on my feet, picked up one paw-paw from the bench
in the kitchen, went quietly out my front door and crossed the
road to the willow tree.

Grandmother Four was sleeping peacefully, stretched out
on her mat directly under her corner of the bridge. I walked
over and stood beside her. Startled, she sprang to her feet.
Smiling, I looked down at her from my superior height. It was
my advantage. I bent a little and peered under the bridge.

"Bagus," I said. "Nice! Kamu suka? You like?"

"Saja, Nonja,"

"Harga berapa? What does it cost?"

She did not answer and her sharp bright little eyes fell to
the dust at her feet. I balanced the paw-paw under her nose.

"Kamu mau tinggal?" I asked her. "You want to stay?"

"Saja, Nonja."

"Baik," I said. "Good."

She glanced up at my face respectfully, stopped and dived
under the bridge and returned with a tiny purse.

"Buah-buahan harga berapa – the fruit, how much is it?"
she asked.

I shook my head and waved away her purse. She thanked me
and the respect remained. We had taken each other's measure.
She was the acknowledged boss of the other grandmothers.
Always the boss accepts a bigger boss. It was a language she
understood. We smiled at one another like conspirators who
plotted on a higher plane than the mere exchange of silver.
She bowed very low.

When I reached my front door, it swung open to welcome
me. Punip was dressed in his white coat and Sura was adding

the finishing touches to a glass of iced coffee to be put on a tray already arranged to receive it. I handed Punip the paw-paw.

"Go and tell the old grandmother with the baby that I forgive her this time. But she must not steal again, nor the other grandmothers. They cannot stay if they steal."

Punip looked very impressed. On his way out he turned at the door.

"There are four paw-paws on the bench in the kitchen, Nonja," he said. "Shall I put them in the refrigerator?"

"You and Sura may take three, if you wish, Punip," I said sweetly.

I knew I was adding another task to an overloaded life but there was already no doubt that the paw-paws would henceforth be laid out daily for my disposal.

It was a funny thing how all our guests in Jakarta gravitated to the balcony to watch the beautiful water-nymphs bathing in the river and never once noticed the four old grandmothers who sat daily under the willow tree.

LITTLE NIPA

In *mid-20th century Indonesia, servants were merely part of the great unskilled and untrained working class who did their best to earn their rice in any capacity the environment and opportunity provided. An industrial society absorbs such people in factories, where they combine in unions to protect their rights, and the law expects the employers to train them adequately to perform their duties. Personal rather than mass employment should work on the same principle, but it is much harder to manipulate on a basis fair to both employer and employed.*

It is a mistake to assume, with righteous indignation, that the downtrodden citizens of newly independent nations suffer as oppressed household servants of richer foreigners. Oppression in the developing countries, democratic or otherwise, has little to do with the foreign population; it exists wherever power-seeking human nature sees an opportunity to take advantage of the economically less fortunate – a class generously found among the nearest neighbours.

In any over-populated country, you are expected to have servants if you belong to an income group which, by the unwritten law of economic distribution, allows you to support them. If you refuse this obligation, even if your accommodation is limited to one room, you are considered anti-social and unwilling to assume your share of the common burden of survival.

It is assumed, of course, that even a person faced with personal service for the first time recognises that under one roof all parties must be suited to exist side by side, although often the time for adjustment is allowed more generously by servants than by their impatient employers. This is natural and the same would occur in an office or a shop. The employer has the greater responsibility, a fact that every employee makes allowances for and accepts, along with everything else the employment offers. The trouble is that very few foreign employers of servants real- ise just how great the responsibility is considered to be by the servant, or just how much the employment offers. In Indonesia, for example, does the employment mean responsibility for your servant's health and food, or the health and food of all his rela- tions? And does your employment offer, for example, the higher status that gives your servant the possibility of considering an- other wife?

If employers are not careful, all privacy can be dispersed by the constant presence of a servant. The master may own the house but the servant cleans it with intimate care and attention dedicated to each separate part, taking account of the master's idiosyncrasies that swell the importance of a servant in village society today as they did in the days of Cervantes' Don Quixote. In Indonesia, the reverse situation is even more tantalising. It is only in embassies and government mansions that, if you don't happen to be an Indonesian citizen, servants' accommodation is provided on the premises. Even then, your servant has a second home in a local kampong and a country village. The villages, though cramped, are delightfully picturesque, but the local kampongs, especially in Jakarta, often suffer from overcrowding and rapid growth. In what all-purpose canal does your servant bathe on his day off before returning to breathe on your bath- room mirror? He does not say, nor does he explain when he asks for an advance on next week's pay why he gambled away last week's substance. Your business is his but his is not yours. He is Doctor Jekyll and Mister Hyde, but you never see Mister Hyde until the result of his doubtful deeds is laid on your doorstep as part of your responsibility.

This is the story of Punip, Sura and little Nipa. Three charming people whom I employed in a home the size of a small apartment with a garden overlooking a river, after the manner expected of me in an over-populated country. I could not, of course, offer a man and his wife and five children accommodation in a backyard tool shed with a corner kept clean for ironing, so they kept on living wherever they were living in an unknown kampong, an unknown distance from my premises. There is no doubt that their status rose in that kampong, wherever it was, on the strength of my employment. Punip became a big man there. I hope he still is, because his stature shrank to a delicate domestic balance, discreetly maintained, from the day I paid Sura a salary placed in her own hands.

~

When we took up residence in Jakarta, Punip and his wife Sura were already established on our premises. As far as I could make out, Punip kept the grounds tidy, the paths swept and the snails squashed during business hours as a part-time preliminary employment prior to cleaning my husband's nearby offices immediately the staff departed. He was a bouncy, barefooted young man, dressed only in a pair of well-washed khaki shorts that he changed twice a day with the fashion-conscious fastidiousness expected of a headwaiter at the Ritz. When he reappeared in the freshly laundered garment his torso shone clean as polished teak and his straight black hair was neatly parted, soaked and plastered to his rather large head. Actually, although he worked in the garden, I never saw Punip dirty on any part of his person, except – of course – his large, flat feet. Yet it was impossible not to notice how he shone when he changed his shorts. Even his black eyes, which I came to call "innocently insolent" had a rinsed gleam in them, and his smile of heavy white teeth sparkled like the inside of a coconut.

Sura, his wife, was a lamp less highly trimmed. A painfully thin little woman, shy and strained, she presented herself to me – with a push through the door from Punip – as a part-time laundress. We had also inherited a houseboy attached as general factotum to the living quarters who seemed incapable of doing anything except stand around with his mouth open, having never before worked for anything so strange as a European woman. I was therefore pleased to give Sura some household linen and tell her to wash it. She took it away to a shed in the corner of the back yard and, with the aid of an old-fashioned flat-iron heated on a tin kerosene stove, laundered it beautifully.

My husband's predecessor had been a bachelor; a club man when he could spare the time from his hobby, which was collecting unusual artefacts. He had travelled locally every week-end to search for rare pieces and, of course, had been absent for weeks at a time on official missions. His requirements in a houseboy naturally differed considerably from mine as even his entertaining had been done at his club. From observation during my first two weeks in Jakarta I surmised that his laundry had been taken care of through Punip, who had arranged for Sura to do it, and that on every other count he had been steadily fleeced by the houseboy.

It is important in the East not to be hasty in your judgements, and important to me to give every human being a fair chance to prove himself, but after Punip had to be called in from the garden to move every piece of furniture and I had cooked every meal, Sura had taken over the personal as well as the household laundry and a member of the office staff delegated to take me shopping, I was forced to the conclusion that the houseboy was, from my point of view, well-paid for doing nothing and also financially prepared to set himself up in business elsewhere. He did not seem surprised and walked out immediately when I worked up the courage to dismiss him. For my part, I was intrigued to see Punip accompany him around the house until he departed; Sura walk him to the side gate, smiling broadly; and the office driver get out of the car to look him over suspiciously as he walked toward the gate with his pay in his hand. Five minutes later I was even more surprised when Punip, with the youngest office secretary beside him to interpret, presented himself as an applicant for the houseboy's job.

To tell the truth, I was not prepared at that moment to receive applicants for any job. I actually had visions of suffering the abominable heat lying on my bed without having to shut the door of the bedroom and so block the draught. I wanted to be absolutely alone in my own house for once. The only possible person I thought I could bear was Sura tiptoeing in the back door to place her bundle of laundry on the kitchen table. I had even considered taking a shower and walking from the bathroom to the bedroom in my petticoat – a cool, delightful thought. I am afraid I was abrupt with Punip. Could he cook, I asked him through the secretary? Had he ever been a houseboy? Could he lay a table? Could he serve drinks?

Punip, changed into his fresh shorts, was as honest as he was clean. No, he could not cook. Cooking was women's work and Sura did his cooking for him. But he could scrub and polish better than the last houseboy, and if that one could serve drinks in a white coat, he could do just as well serving drinks in a white coat. He wanted to better himself by working as the boss's houseboy because the boss's houseboy got more money than he at present received. He wanted to work for me because I let Sura launder my clothes and it was good for a man and his wife with five children to support at school, to work in the same place and see each other every day.

I looked at Punip with a new respect in the light of his youthful appearance considering he was the father of five school-age children. I felt I also understood the rather more prominent lines that graced Sura's tiny face. I told the secretary to tell Punip I would speak with my husband about his suggestion. There was also the part-time gardening to consider, and the office cleaning. Punip's enthusiasm was in no way dimmed. Would I please tell the tuan that he, with the help of Sura, would manage all three jobs until a replacement was found, and that he had a friend who was a houseboy who would teach him English for serving at table and passing out drinks in a white coat. I smiled at Punip with all the dignity I could muster against the proximity of that white coat that I would buy and Sura launder. He grinned at me like an impudent child and then he bowed in exact imitation of the newly departed houseboy's one and only condescension.

As soon as Punip and his interpreter closed the door behind them, I took my cold shower and then walked slowly in the air-stir from all the open doors along the hall from the bathroom to the bedroom in my petticoat. For the first time all day, I felt degrees cooler and unexpectedly cheerful. A tiny knock sounded on the door behind me, and I turned to find Sura standing with her eyes lowered on a tray holding a tall glass of icedcoffee and a large plate decorated with two small almond-macaroon biscuits.

"Iced coffee?" I said. "How nice! I didn't know you could make iced coffee. Thank you."

"T'ank you," Sura whispered with her eyes down. "Ice koppie! I look, you make."

I took the tray from her and, as I did so, she looked up. Her eyes were very large and dark and knowing as they smiled shyly up into my own. Then she turned and fled.

~

The next morning, I put my proposition to Punip. I would employ him along with his wife Sura as a couple. Punip would clean the house every morning and serve at table and parties in a white coat when we had guests. Sura would do the laundry in the morning and I would teach her to cook European meals. In the afternoon, Sura could go home to her children in the kampong from three to six, and need not come back when we were dining out. My husband was willing that Punip retain his gardening job for the office, which could be done in the afternoon until time to slip on his white coat if guests arrived. A replacement would be found to do the office cleaning who could also be a guard on the premises all night.

Now, this was not exactly a conventional arrangement for our circumstances, and in proposing it, I knew I was going against the freely-offered advice of the local European and American population who swore that a previously-trained houseboy was essential. I reasoned that because of my ignorance of local conditions, I would probably be in for a household re-shuffle in a few months anyway, as I had already guessed that even the purveyors of the most proven advice, offered with the maximum experience, seemed to undergo a servant crisis with predictable regularity. I thought I would try a settling-in period of reasonable household security on my own terms, which included the hot afternoon to myself within my limited space. As far as I could judge, the office staff approved ofPunip. He was cheerful, ambitious and willing to learn. I found his wife quite charming, apart altogether from her work as a laundress and the fact that she could learn without being told, by the "I look" method, which I felt was a great advantage. Surely, I had argued with myself the previous evening in the presence of my husband, such an arrangement would work at least until after our daughters came for the Christmas holidays. How, I asked, could Punip get too big for his new white coat, as predicted by numerous European advisers, in that short time? My husband, with wise male magnanimity, gave his full support to any decision I decided to make on the household front. He agreed under pressure that my proposition would be good if it worked. He had staff problems of his own he was waiting to discuss in the light of his forthcoming mission to Japan, and I did not find it difficult to discern that the replacement of Punip as the office cleaner was the least of them.

Punip accepted my proposition immediately on behalf of himself and on behalf of Sura, who was neither consulted, nor present during the negotiations. However, he explained through the office secretary, he had two provisos, which he impressed upon his interpreter I must understand had nothing whatever to do with work. I had named a salary to be paid to himself and a salary to be paid to Sura. As the head of his family, he would like both salaries to be paid to him. A little staggered, I listened to his second provision. His favourite daughter, little Nipa, whom I may have noticed sitting in the laundry-shed while her mother was working, was delicate. If Sura worked in the house, little Nipa would have to sit in the house. Under no circumstances could he allow little Nipa to be out of his sight in the kampong with the old grandmothers.

I compromised. If little Nipa only sat in the kitchen or played in the garden, I was not against her coming with her mother, at least until I saw how such a scheme would work out. On the other hand, women in my country were personally paid for the work they did and I preferred to pay Sura her own salary. Punip's eyes flashed a shrewd, calculating flitter before the concession to little Nipa won the day. Then he grinned and departed to fetch the scrubbing bucket.

On that day, little Nipa moved into my kitchen.

~

From the beginning, the arrangement with Punip and Sura worked very well. Punip had the honour of keeping the floors and furniture polished with the glint of a new tin can.

Honouring the new white coat was harder for him, but even in his most awkward moment he tried hard, and finally succeeded when he gave up wearing slippers, which proved a hazard past endurance. Sura looked him over back and front when he showered and donned his coat to serve at drinks or dinner, and allowed no speck of dust to darken his leathery feet, so he took to wearing his slippers outside in the evening when he was on duty. His slippers, a rather wide pair of carpet-bag strapped sandals took up a permanent position at the kitchen door.

As the boss-tuan's houseboy, Punip considered himself under my orders for the garden between the office and the river, which was really only mine by proxy in working hours, except as a part of the view from the balcony. Punip was as tidy in the garden as he was in the house, but re-arrangement and innovation was outside his province. If, however, I suggested a shrub should be trimmed, a tree shaped or a flowerbed planted, he beamed with approval and set to work. Cohorts of enormous snails and battalions of black ants opposed our efforts, and often a tropical storm would wipe out in five minutes the whole afternoon's work, but improvements were gradually consolidated with the help of tropical growth in the humid greenhouse atmosphere. Before very long the river view was framed with red poinsettia, pink and yellow frangipani, enormous tangerine and scarlet hibiscus blossoms. Punip grew very proud of the garden. One morning he put down his duster to step out on the balcony to gloat. The soft voice of Sura, calling his name, deprived him of his moment of arrogance. I was sitting writing in my corner chair on the balcony and Sura was carefully conscious of the proprieties.

It was not until after I began to teach English to Indonesian ladies, and could therefore prove I had tasted and enjoyed Indonesian food, that Sura could be persuaded to prepare it for me. After about six weeks of struggling to copy my unfamiliar methods of preparing steak and vegetables, fish in batter and

Spanish omelette, she suddenly relaxed and, left to her own devices, produced an excellent nasi goreng, with krupuk, fried prawns and bananas. The next day she served a chicken casserole, which was delicious, and the following a fish baked in bamboo after her own fashion. It was my turn to relax. She had learned to prepare daily my kind of tropical fruit salad; wash the imported lettuce and the local tomatoes and fruit; boil and refrigerate the drinking water, and prepare half a dozen meals with enough variety to satisfy our taste. I knew that I would have to make special occasion food myself under her watchful "look-see-you-make" eyes. I also realised that, although she did not understand my reasons as other than strangely foreign, her kitchen hygiene would be carried out scrupulously because I wanted it that way. And she was quiet and soft-spoken in the home.

But she was not so quiet as her daughter little Nipa. Little Nipa was so quiet you could mistake her for a doll. She looked like a display doll, with enormous, flat, black velvet eyes lashed with curled silk and a face of smooth yellow parchment under a straight black fringe of hair.

While her mother was inside, little Nipa sat beside her father's slippers at the kitchen door. As soon as I entered the kitchen, she disappeared from my sight to sit one down on the outside steps. At first, I made the usual overtures, smiling at her, and offering a biscuit or a sweet. She would look at me solemnly with eyes as wide and uncomprehending as a bushbaby's or an owl caught in the glare of a flashlight. Then her little round mouth would tremble and the suspicion of tears rim her lashes. She would shake her head almost unperceptively towards my offering and, rather than make her cry, I would leave her on the step. After all, I told myself, I was strange to her and it could be that she was extraordinarily shy. Also, I suspected that her presence being one of her parents' conditions of employment, she had been warned to keep out of my way, which may have frightened her, not unnaturally. I decided to make no fuss of the child for a week or two so she could get used to me. After that, I tried to speak to her again but the response was just the same. This time I felt somehow rebuffed and, straightening up, went back into the kitchen where I made it plain to Sura that it was not necessary for Nipa to leave as soon as I came near. Sura studied my face as I spoke, her eyes perplexed and sombre. Then she nodded. The next time I went into the kitchen little Nipa did not move but sat with her hands folded listlessly in her lap. I smiled at her but she gazed back at me as blankly as ever. After that, she was always in the kitchen.

By this time the social life of Jakarta had assumed demanding proportions. I was enjoying new friendships through my English class, and had begun to remember through familiarity of use, a few phrases of the Bahasa Indonesian language. My husband was about to go to Japan on a mission, and after his return our children would join us for Christmas. With some time to myself in the afternoons, I was learning to live with the humid heat. In fact, I was settling down amiably, with all my senses alert to get the very most I could from every new experience. I did not realise how much of my amiability depended upon the assumption that Punip and Sura were also settling down. Nor, unfortunately, did my subconscious calculations adequately estimate the power of little Nipa.

It was not that I ignored her presence in my house, far from it. She upset me, and I knew it positively from the day I began to give Sura instructions for the day's meals at the breakfast table instead of going to the kitchen. What I did not know was that Punip and Sura knew it, and worse than that, argued and finally fought about it. I knew Punip worshipped little Nipa. I had a few inquiries of the office staff who spoke English. Nobody knew what was the matter with the child. She was just delicate, they said. Had she always been delicate?

No, apparently only the last year or so. Had they ever seen her smile? Oh yes, she always smiled when she saw her father, but with everybody else, she was very shy. Did they ever see her play? Oh no, she was too delicate to play. Were the other children in the family delicate as well? Oh no, they were all very healthy and went to school. Every answer was non-committal and non-involved and typical of a safe reply for a new boss's wife.

So, the day arrived when I drove to the airport to see my husband off to Japan. After his departure, I spent a little time looking at carvings in the curio shop and, on my way out, saw a little American kewpie doll displayed incongruously with others of its kind in a box near the door. It had a pink face, a frilly net skirt, a blue hair-ribbon and a pair of tinsel wings. On an impulse I bought it for Nipa and put it in my handbag.

The office driver was waiting for me and we walked together the short distance to the car. He was a courteous man who always took the trouble speak to me slowly in Bahasa, which I appreciated as complimentary to my efforts to learn the language. Speaking very carefully I asked him a question. "Do you know what is the matter with little Nipa?" I realised as I put the phrases together that I must have been practicing them in my mind, and would not have to repeat myself to make him understand. He stepped back as if I had asked him to drive the car into the canal, only recovering in time to open the car door. After I stepped in, he closed the door, bowed, opened his own door and slipped behind the steering wheel. But he did not start the car. Instead, he stared straight out the windscreen and made a short clear speech which somehow shook me to the marrow. He began by declaring his faith in Allah as a good Muslim. I could not miss that, after all the years I had lived in the Muslim world. Then he said something about Punip and the kampong and a 'si Bodoh' which I thought meant a stupid one or a fool. Then he mentioned little Nipa in the same sentence as a large amount of money. When he finished, he did not repeat a word or ask if I understood, which I did not. There was nothing I could do except say, "Terima kasi", which is "Thank you", and drive home in silence.

It was a little after five in the afternoon. We had lunched at home before leaving for the airport and I was dining out with friends for dinner. On my return, I expected Punip to be in the garden and Sura long since departed to her kampong with the rest of the day off. Instead, Punip was nowhere to be seen and I found Sura waiting to open the front door and little Nipa sitting in her usual place in the kitchen. It was hot, so I accepted Sura's suggestion of an iced coffee before I asked why she had not gone home. She indicated, with hesitation, that she preferred not to go home but to sleep on the kitchen floor while the tuan was away. I shook my head. The new guard was on duty, I told her, and I was perfectly safe. She must go home and sleep with her children and take little Nipa with her.

For the first time since she had worked in my house, Sura began to argue with me. I could not follow the speed of the words that rushed from her throat in a torrent of pleading, broken phrases, punctuated by a pause after several questions that I could not answer. Yet I recognised odd words, some of them the same as those used by the driver like "much money" and "little Nipa and Punip" spoken in the same breath.

At last, I said, "Where is Punip?"

She shook her head and shrugged.

"Should I get the secretary from the office to translate?"

"No, no." She shook her head with agitated violence. Then we looked at each other and something she expected of me collapsed in Sura and she gave up, her eyes deadened to expressionless acceptance of defeat. She had failed to make me understand and sat suddenly like a whipped animal on the floor beside little Nipa. Nervously exhausted, frustrated with the inadequacy of language, I gave in. After all, she was not asking much, only to sleep on the kitchen floor. "Stay tonight." I told her. "Tomorrow I'll see."

I sighed audibly as I left the kitchen. I knew I had done the wrong thing. Sura could not be allowed to sleep on the kitchen floor, let alone the child. Language difficulties notwithstanding, I understood enough to realise my action had interfered to support Sura in a domestic struggle with her husband over little Nipa, which had something to do with money. At that time, I suspected that, prior to her employment in my house, Sura would never have dared to oppose Punip. I even felt guilty about the children in the kampong whom I had never seen and wondered if, like little Nipa, they wouldn't even smile at me if I ever did meet them. Downstairs, the office staff were busily employed adjusting themselves to the orders of the second-in-command, whom I knew little better than they did. I felt no desire to seek advice from that quarter. Nor, upon reflection under the shower, did I think I would feel inclined to ask the opinion of any of the guests at the dinner party I was about to attend. I wished briefly that my acquaintance with some of the Indonesian members of my English class had progressed as far as personal friendship. Time definitely was not on my side.

In the end, as I might have known from the beginning, I did nothing. Even worse than that, I blithely announced to the friends who brought me home that they need not come in with me as my maid was sleeping in for a night or two until I got used to being alone. I did not say where she was sleeping. The hall light was on, my bed turned down, and the door to the kitchen wide open. Sura and little Nipa were sleeping peacefully in their clothes on a rattan mat in the corner where Punip housed his slippers.

As might be expected, I was awakened in the morning after a restless night by more than birds. A lively argument was in progress at the back door. I put on my dressing gown and went to shower. My appearance in the hall had the desired effect.

Punip went down the back steps and Sura inside to the re-frigerator to start preparations for my breakfast. Ten minutes later, eating my daily fruit salad of pamplemousses, paw-paw, pineapple and bananas, I noticed Sura was newly bathed, with her sleek, wet hair beautifully arranged in a coil at the back of her neck, and wearing a fresh sarong and white muslin blouse. Her face looked relaxed, her eyes and lips smiled. She even wore a pair of neat, cork-soled slippers on her tiny feet, which made a subdued but definite little clop as she moved around. I was forced to wonder if she had enjoyed her first good night's sleep for some time on my kitchen floor. As Sura brought in my coffee, Punip entered the hall from the kitchen with his scrubbing brush and bucket. For the next hour until the office opened at eight o'clock, he worked steadily without raising his head. When even the kitchen floor shone like a mirror under the feet of Sura and little Nipa, he went down the back steps.

In the mornings I wrote my letters on my balcony where the early hours were shaded cool and the river view enchant-ing. I had a polished board on hinges that let down above my knees like a small table from the wall beside the last rattan chair. It was my favourite corner and Punip knew I was to be found there when he returned with the little office secretary to interpret for him once more.

"Punip has a request to make," this little lady informed me, smugly standing in the minute available space. "Punip would like for you to give him pay for next week now, please."

Beside her, Punip beamed assent. He had put on his white coat and looked very clean.

"Tell Punip I cannot grant his request. I will not have the money to pay him until the end of the week."

She did not bother to translate this to Punip.

"Oh, that will be OK," she informed me brightly. "You can write a note to the office and the accountant will pay."

I looked at the girl, small and perky with her Western linen dress, permed hair and white sandals and began to understand my husband's staff problems.

"Please tell Punip," I repeated, smiling at her sweetly, "that he will not be borrowing money from the office."

Now what, I wondered, as the girl pushed Punip aside a little to get back into the lounge-room, speaking rapidly to him in Bahasa, none of which I could understand except that it was considerably more, and much more vehement, than the few words I had uttered.

Finally, I heard a rapid exchange of male and female voices from my kitchen before the front door closed after the little secretary who would not, of course, demean herself by walking down the back steps. For perhaps five minutes I stared contemplatively at the river running fast and swollen with mountain rain through the city to the sea. It was still rather soon after breakfast for the glass of iced coffee Sura placed on my table without speaking a word, departing as she had come like a silent conspirator. But she was back again very soon and her whole demeanour had changed. Nervously, she announced that Mr Tong wished to see me.

Now, Mr Tong was the office accountant and, except for the international staff, the senior man in the office. Mr Tong did the banking and the salaries on the local level. He spoke and wrote English, Dutch, Chinese and Bahasa with equal and precise facility. My husband, unlike some of his overseas colleagues, was not in favour of disposing of the services of Mr Tong, even though he was forced to agree that getting information from Mr Tong beyond the impeccably kept figures in the account books, was like probing the secrets of a lunar operation. Mr Tong, in other words, was my husband's staff problem at the head of the list. I was filled with wonder that Mr Tong should wish to see me. Not that he was ever anything but polite and helpful when we met, but because my husband had arranged for him to cash my cheque at the end of the week and Mr Tong was said to be rigid to the point of immovability when it came to carrying out instructions. Besides, Mr Tong had never before been in my house, even to see my husband, without the previous use of the telephone. So, I left my chair on the balcony and greeted Mr Tong in the lounge. He came to the point immediately.

"Madame," he said, "I hope you will excuse me if I have disturbed you. But it has just come to my ears that you wish to cash a cheque and do not feel free to approach me in the matter until the arranged appointment day. I would be failing in my duty, Madame, if I allowed you to continue under such a misapprehension. During your husband's absence, I am at your disposal at any time."

I stared in surprise at Mr Tong and sat down on the nearest chair.

"Please sit down, Mr Tong," I said. "It is most kind of you to come. But you have been misinformed. I do not wish to cash a cheque and if I did, I assure you I would certainly make use of your kind services. Why ever should I not?"

Mr Tong did not wish to sit down but he did, on the very edge of the chair facing my own. Nor did he wish to answer my question, so I waited.

"Madame," he said at last. "I offer my apologies."

"There is no need for you to apologise. But I feel that perhaps you and I have a problem. Mine, as you will readily understand with your obvious gift for languages, is the difficulty of being misinterpreted, yours perhaps, of being misinformed of my purpose."

Not a muscle moved in his immobile face but a tiny spark glittered in his eyes.

"Madame?" he questioned, and he waited.

"I would like to ask you a question. Did Punip try to borrow money from his future office salary as a gardener?"

"I refused his request, Madame, naturally, during your husband's absence."

"Both Mr Horst and Mr Johnstone could have given you permission."

"I preferred not to ask them, Madame, as the request was unjustified."

"In what way?"

He hesitated and then looked at me strangely as if he saw me for the first time in the light of some face he had just remembered. Immediately he asked me a question.

"Punip made the same request of you, Madame?"

"Yes, and like you I refused him, but not, I feel sure, for the same reasons. I am being frank with you, Mr Tong, because I trust this matter will rest only between our two selves – in my husband's absence."

He said quickly and I believed him:"I assure you, Madame, your confidence is justified. I do not know the reason you refused to give Punip this money and believe me, I am embarrassed to refuse to divulge the reason for my refusal. If I did, Madame, I would jeopardise Punip's service with you, and that, to my sure knowledge, is more important to him than the money. He is a foolish man but not about your services, Madame."

"I would not have thought, Mr Tong, that my service is more important to Punip than little Nipa."

Mr Tong's solemn face twitched.

"Then you know, Madame, why Punip wants the money and Sura will not give it to him?"

"Sura?"

"If Sura had been willing to give Punip the money, he would have had no need to ask for it."

"But where would Sura get it?"

"She has saved it, Madame, and, I understand, hidden it. As long as Sura keeps the money, Punip cannot take the child back to the kampong for the ceremony."

"But I understand that Punip will not allow little Nipa to be left in the kampong."

"Oh no, Madame. In this you have been misinformed. Sura will not let the child out of her sight. She believes the child might be killed, not cured."

"Mr Tong, do you know what is wrong with the child?"

"Nobody knows, Madame. She was chosen for the Legong dances before she sickened. Punip was very proud. He is a big man in the kampong. The people there say Sura put a spell on the child because Punip went with another woman. That is why he must pay for the ceremony, Madame, to break the spell."

Quite suddenly I realised I had learned enough for one day and that, if I kept on, Mr Tong would feel obliged to tell me what the ceremony was and I did not want to know. It was quite enough that he disapproved of it and Sura was terrified it would kill little Nipa. I stood up.

Mr Tong rose to his feet and we faced each other at a loss for words. Yet, in that moment, a bond was established between us that lasted with mutual benefit throughout the whole of my stay in Indonesia.

"Thank you, Mr Tong," I said at last. "I quite appreciate your reluctance to discuss the personal affairs of the staff. I approve of your attitude, which is my own."

"I am Chinese, Madame."

"Yes, Mr Tong, I know."

"You may rest assured I will handle the matter of my mis-information without disclosure, if that is your wish, Madame."

"Thank you, Mr Tong, I would prefer that."

I had an impulse to ask him where he had learned his English but refrained. Our relationship was, in both time and opportunity, too young. He bowed and I allowed him to depart.

~

I was meeting my French friends for drinks at the club in the late afternoon and dining informally at their home. For Punip and Sura it was considered a night off, and I knew my friend Jacques would easily be persuaded to bring me home early. Therefore, it seemed reasonable to wait until after lunch to tell Sura she could not sleep in the kitchen again. I presumed Sura had hidden her money somewhere in one of my cupboards. Apparently, as long as she had it, her personal insurance was adequate. Jacques was an old friend from pre-Jakarta days and it would be perfectly natural to ask him casually what he knew about magic spells and ceremonies as practiced for a price in the kampongs.

Having worked out my little speech for Sura from the Bahasa phrase book and written it out several times with pencil and paper, I nevertheless answered Sura's call to luncheon with trepidation. Then I remembered the doll I had bought for little Nipa that waited, forgotten, in my handbag. Now, I thought, before I sit down to lunch, is the time to present it.

Sura was removing a small casserole from the oven. I walked across the kitchen behind her and held out the kewpie doll to little Nipa. It was a moment of miracle. The child's eyes shone, her lips parted over even white teeth, the front two of which I noticed with astonishment were second teeth. She snatched the doll and clasped it tight in her tiny hands, her arms held out like wooden sticks to receive it. Sura dropped the casserole with a bang on the sink and ran to stand beside little Nipa, her dark eyes full of terrible excitement.

"You like Nipa, you like?" she demanded of me.

Astonished at her question, I nodded my head. Sura relaxed and together we stared down at little Nipa holding the kewpie doll. It was then I saw the spot, no more than a damp bloody pinhead on Nipa's dress under her raised arm. I bent down and very gently lifted her elbow a little higher, and saw plainly a small, ugly sore. How could I have been so stupid not to have suspected the possibility before. Little Nipa had yaws.

A great surge of relief swept through me.

"Go and get Mr Tong," I said to Sura. "Go and get Mr Tong."

Sura shook with a new fear. "Sec-re-tary?" she whispered, "Nonja want sec-re-tary talk?"

"No, not secretary, Mr Tong. Get Mr Tong."

She went down the back stairs.

Little Nipa watched her go, looked at the doll, looked at me, smiled – but only slightly, slumped against the wall and sat with her back against it on the floor. The doll, released from her bird-like grip, fell from her. She retrieved it and held it loosely on her knee, staring at it vacantly, emotionless. A great lump rose in my throat. All for a single shot of penicillin, one injection of penicillin!

"Madame?"

"Mr Tong. I believe I have just found out what is the matter with little Nipa. She has yaws, that's all. She has yaws. I will phone UNICEF to arrange for penicillin. I know somebody there. We can get it done right away. It only takes one injection, I understand. I don't know why it didn't strike me before – because Punip and Sura are so clean, I suppose."

Mr Tong did not appear to share my enthusiasm.

"Are you quite sure, Madame?"

"Oh, yes, I think so. I had the sores pointed out to me at the hospital clinic, and I have seen UN photographs. I want you to tell Sura for me, Mr Tong, that I believe I have found out what is the sickness of Nipa and that I will arrange to have her cured right away."

Mr Tong said, "If you wish it, Madame. But neither Punip nor Sura will agree to the needle; that being the reason they gave when I suggested they take the little girl to see a doctor. They expect she will die if given a needle."

"But that is ridiculous. Why should she die from a shot of penicillin? It only takes one injection of penicillin to cure a case of yaws."

"So I heard, Madame, but the people in the kampongs are led to believe otherwise. I am sorry to upset you, Madame, but many children die in the kampongs. The death of children is almost a daily occurrence. They blame the needle."

"Just the same, Mr Tong, I must ask you to tell Sura that little Nipa must have an injection of penicillin. My children are coming here for Christmas holidays. Even if they were not, I could not watch little Nipa sit day after day like that in my kitchen, knowing she could be cured. Tell Sura. I think she will understand."

But I knew as I watched Sura's face while Mr Tong translated that she did not understand. She looked stricken and her eyes filled with tears. Mr Tong repeated with patience all he had said a second time. Sura began to tremble but she did not speak a word or ask one question. Only her head dropped forward suddenly, so that I could not see her face while her small thin body shook like a leaf in the wind.

"Sura," I said, "Sura, what's wrong with you? Are you ill?Apa-kamu-sakit? Are you ill?"

Mr Tong spoke. "She is not ill, Madame. She is frightened."

"Please tell her there is nothing to be frightened of, Mr Tong. Tell her I would do exactly the same if Nipa was my own child. Tell her I am sure little Nipa will get better, that I like little Nipa and want her to get better, that I will go with her myself to get the injection."

The face of Mr Tong wore an expression of stoical resignation to my whim as he translated my remarks to Sura. I realised that my last words were emotional, my knowledge of local conditions inadequate, and that if I did not terminate the scene in my kitchen, I would lose the respect I had somehow aroused in Mr Tong. I felt awkward and slightly ill myself, but in no way less determined that little Nipa must have an injection. I did not give Sura a chance to lift her head and reply to me through Mr Tong, even supposing she showed the inclination. The moment Mr Tong finished speaking I told him something else to tell Sura. He was to say that the conversation between us was not to be mentioned to anyone else and that Sura was to stay in the kitchen and think about her job and little Nipa until I returned after dinner in the evening. I would like her to put my lunch on the table in five minutes and then when I finished, I would be having a rest until I went out. I knew this cancelled out the little speech I had prepared in Bahasa telling Sura she could not sleep again in the kitchen, but I had forgotten it anyway and made thankfully for the door.

An unexpected small voice piped up.

"Nonja?"

I swung around. I had never heard little Nipa speak before. The child was smiling at me with the doll clutched tight in her arms. I almost choked as I forced myself to smile back.

"Terima kasi, Nonja, saja suka," little Nipa said, which simply translated means "Thank you, Madame, I like."

~

As I suspected, my friend Jacques had absorbed considerable information about incantations, killing of cocks, magic spells and financial exhortation as practiced in the environs of Jakarta. He had a friend who had found his trousers and a few unmentionables under his servant's mattress after an argument and another friend whose houseboy had withered away and died because of a spell. Jacques had a witty tongue that responded with sardonic glee to the challenge of detail and anecdote on the victims of superstition. After about ten minutes, his wife, Martine, reminded him that I was alone in my flat, that she found the heat enough to contend with in the night, and if it was not too much to ask, would he kindly change the subject. Once again, on my return home, I was glad to be able to say that my hosts need not worry about me as Sura was waiting to let me in.

Sura, with little Nipa beside her, was sound asleep on my kitchen floor.

~

There is, of course, a limit to the amount of sleep you can do without, as well as a limit in the opposite direction. I was sleeping soundly in spite of the noise of the traffic when Sura brought me in a glass of iced coffee at eight o'clock in the morning. She put it on my bedside table, made sure I was alive to drink it, and ran out again. Work in the office had already begun, Punip had finished the living-room floor, and Mr Tong had sent a message wishing to see me by the time I had showered. I sat down to my breakfast without the slightest enthusiasm to face the day. I glanced at Sura speculatively and found her looking more refreshed than I felt myself. She even suggested her chicken dish for lunch and when I agreed, departed to the kitchen with a look of satisfaction. When the table was cleared, I sent Punip for Mr Tong.

Punip, Mr Tong informed me, had been waiting for his arrival at the office and wished him to tell me that he had arranged his affairs without the loan and was sorry to have bothered me about it.

"Has he given up the ceremony to cure little Nipa, then?"

"He did not say so, Madame. He said he was advised his job was more important."

"Did Sura tell him?"

"He would not take advice from Sura. He is a big man in his kampong. I imagine he took advice from the friend who advised him that as such a big man he should apply for the job as your houseboy, Madame."

"Would you say, Mr Tong, that his friend believed in the ceremony to cure little Nipa?"

"I could not say, Madame, but I think the friend would be unable to openly support it."

"So Punip supported the friend instead of little Nipa?"

"The friend said little Nipa could not possibly get worse if kept out of the kampong to sit in your kitchen. The friend does not live in the kampong, Madame."

I realise that, Mr Tong," I said lightly. "Do you think Sura knows the influence of this friend?"

"Yes, Madame."

"Has Sura spoken to you this morning, Mr Tong?"

"No, Madame."

"Do you think she has spoken to Punip?"

"No, Madame."

"Then I think, Mr Tong, we will call them both in now while you are here to translate for me. It is better, don't you think, than Punip calling the secretary from downstairs to speak for him?"

Mr Tong did not reply.

~

Punip, who really was a handsome specimen, stood straight as a tree with his face and torso shining like old copper and a glint in his black eyes. Sura stood beside him like a wary, wide-eyed spaniel about to be hit. Punip looked at Mr Tong and Sura's eyes were magnetised in fear on my face.

I asked Mr Tong to tell Punip that I was very grateful to be told that he had taken the advice of his friend and decided against borrowing money from his salary. I wanted him to know, because I was very satisfied with his work so far and was sure that with time and experience, he would make an excellent houseboy. Mr Tong translated. Punip beamed his acceptance of the compliment. A tiny spark flashed in Sura's eyes. Then I asked Mr Tong to tell Sura that I was very pleased with her work as both cook and laundress, and hoped she would continue in my service, providing of course that she was willing to have little Nipa injected for yaws. Mr Tong translated.

Punip scarcely waited for Mr Tong to finish before he shot out a series of questions, which Mr Tong answered with the same sharp tone. The short exchange sounded like the blast of a machine gun. Then Punip turned to Sura and spoke his mind. Sura lowered her eyes and bowed her head as a good wife should.

"Well?" I asked Mr Tong before Punip's wrath was fully exercised.

"He is saying, Madame, that if Sura agrees to Nipa having an injection, he will publicly divorce her in the kampong, and that if he does that, she will never see her children again and that she won't even have little Nipa because Nipa will die after the needle. It is the usual threat, Madame."

"When you get a chance, Mr Tong, tell Punip that I do not believe in threats and that I leave the decision entirely up to Sura, who knows now that in modern society children do not die from a needle unless they are taken to get it too late to save their lives anyway. Say also that I know it is not too late to save Nipa and that she will grow up into a beautiful girl if Sura agrees to take her."

My voice had already silenced Punip, who turned abruptly toward Mr Tong to listen with arrogant politeness to what he had to translate. He shrugged and spoke briefly when Mr Tong finished.

"Punip says Sura is his wife and not a modern woman and he does not want her to be. It is enough that he is a modern man."

"Ask Punip why, if he is a modern man, he does not wish Sura to be a modern woman and a modern mother for his children?"

"Punip says Sura does not give him the money she earns and will not do what he tells her to do."

"Tell Punip in that case Sura is already a modern woman and it is very good for his children if she saves her money and will not give it to him to spend on a useless cure for little Nipa."

When Mr Tong translated this, the eyes of Punip and those of his wife swung from his face to mine and then, in comprehensive astonishment, met the eyes of each other. Very sweetly, almost with meekness, Sura smiled at Punip. Amazed I saw Punip bare his large white teeth and smile back. He was still smiling broadly when he addressed himself to Mr Tong. It was then Mr Tong's turn to be surprised, although he did his best not to show it to either party, as a good interpreter should.

"Punip wishes me to tell you, Madame, that he agrees that you are the one who knows the truth of who is modern and who is not, and which cure is modern and which is not. He will tell his relatives in the kampong that you have the same magic for little Nipa that you have for the planting. After little Nipa is cured, Sura can go home again at night from your kitchen to the kampong and he will sleep for your protection in the garden until the tuan returns."

I felt very tempted to collapse into the nearest chair. Instead, I thanked Mr Tong, dismissed Punip graciously as I could, and was left facing Sura who did not depart with the men, but stood hesitantly, just inside the door. She had not spoken once during the whole interview and proceeded to make up for her silence.

"You want – I-ees koppie?" she announced. "You want – I-ee get."

That being the extent of her English, she finished what she had to say in slow Bahasa which she repeated word by word until I understood and could give her an answer.

"Kapan – Nipa – berpakaian – djalan – rumah sakit? Ke-marin – saja – beli – pakaian baru – Nipa – berpakaian – tidak takut" which meant in my literal translation: "When Nipa dress to go to hospital? Yesterday I buy new clothes to dress Nipa – not afraid."

Incredulously, I nodded my head to prove my comprehen-sion and stared at Sura, whose black eyes gazed back into my own with shining candour. Both of us were very close to hysterical laughter.

"Bring a coffee, please," I said quickly, "then I will tele-phone."

And I made for the sanctuary of my balcony, but not before I heard a suppressed giggle from the kitchen, drowned imme-diately by the tap water pouring into the kettle.

~

Little Nipa remained in her seat on the kitchen floor for two days following her injection of penicillin. On the third day she brought iced coffee as I sat writing on my balcony. Her little hands were steady with the tray and her smile sweet. The next day I saw her doing the rounds of the garden with her father, and after that every afternoon she began to play with her doll under the sugar-palm that rose as high as my balcony. A week later I looked down and saw her dancing.

I was told by Mr Tong that Punip became an even bigger man in the kampong, for his was the voice that proclaimed the modern magic of a newly discovered injection that did not kill children. Also, he worked for a nonja whose eyes detected with the speed of a hawk the need for a magic cure. Unfortunately, from my point of view, Punip had a great many relatives in the kampong who proved anxious to benefit from the glance of an eye so peculiarly blessed. I will say for Punip that he thoroughly approved of Sura's suggestion that all candidates expecting therapeutic advice must arrive in my kitchen spotlessly clean, particularly about the legs and feet. For this purpose, Punip made good use of a large, red bar of strong-smelling disinfectant soap and a sharp bristled scrubbing brush, which lay in wait for the unsuspecting beside a bucket underneath the garden water-tap. Once in a while I was thrilled to send a child to be cured of yaws, but usually all that was required to uphold Punip's reputation as a big man in the kampong was some bright red mercurochrome, a package of Conde's Crystals and a constant supply of fascinating Band-Aids.

Finally, I must add that, one by one, all the children of Punip and Sura turned up with big smiles and a need for attention. As they were all boys built in the brash image of Punip, and showed loving respect for Sura and adored little Nipa, I adopted them without trepidation. After all, upholding a reputation for a magic eye and the free distribution of Band-Aids was a small price to pay for devoted service, graciously offered during the whole of my stay in Jakarta. One way and another, I owed a lot to little Nipa.

LAUGHTER

Indonesian traffic rarely evokes laughter. Certainly, for me, even minor amusement was nervously relegated to realms beyond the conscious mind until one day, when I drove in purposeful and concentrated silence behind my tense driver, across Merdeka Square in the centre of Jakarta. On that day, believe me, my reaction was anything but mirthful when the heat of a Java noon entered like a blast from a steam jet through the driver's window, as he suddenly braked less than a yard from the spinning wheels of an over-turned betjak.

As we stopped, another betjak, undamaged and upright, spun to a halt two yards further on, and as my eyes fell on it the bemused passenger stepped out, shaken but unhurt, to the pavement. In the same instant, the passenger from the over-turned vehicle suddenly sat up, dazed and dusty, beside my driver's door. All this happened in a flicker of time. All heavy traffic managed to pull up and no car, fortunately, had suffered the common complaint of slipped brake linings. Nobody seemed seriously hurt. I relaxed. In five minutes we would be on our way again after a non-serious, minor accident, on the overcrowded thoroughfare of the busy square.

Yet by the time these facts had registered, and my driver could step out to assist the sitting betjak passenger to his feet, pandemonium had broken loose. The betjak-drivers had thrown themselves at one another in violent anger and a yelling, jeering crowd surrounded them as suddenly and unexpectedly as djinns from an Aladdin's bottle. Directly in front of our wind-screen the two men were wrestling in fury, already encouraged by the screams of an increasing mob. The up-turned betjak was hard against our bumper bar before my driver had shoved its passenger under our steering wheel, pushed in himself, and closed the door. Both men and myself instinctively ran the car windows up and then the three of us sat in stifling heat, sweating as we stared at the battle.

For a long minute, we watched the struggling betjak-drivers, one up and one down, their naked brown torsos glistening with sweat like gold in the sun. Then the crowd surged closer, climbing on the mud guards of the cars, screaming like excited demons, their arms and legs and heads bobbling up and down between us and the combatants. The little man in our front seat who had been the passenger leaned forward and pressed his brown wrinkled face, under his incongruously tilted black velvet pillbox hat, against the windscreen. But his breath fur-ther hazed his view and he sat back again.

Then my driver, who was taller, cried out, "A knife! One has a knife."

And as he spoke the crowd fell back, pushing those behind in one instinctive movement. There was a sudden eerie silence followed by a long, penetrating hiss. The space around the antagonists was as safely cleared as a boxing arena, and once again we had an unpremeditated ringside seat.

Immediately, and before I realised his intention, the little man in our front seat opened the door and stepped out.

I gasped and cried:"Don't let him out!"

But he was out, and you had to be there to believe what happened. You had to see that little man, no more than five feet tall with his white suit rumpled and streaked with dust and grease and his black pillbox hat askew. You had to see him throw back his head and begin to laugh, loud and harsh, beside that up-turned betjak. His white teeth flashed and his laugh cackled like an ancient hen laying an unexpected egg. The surprised crowd let him walk straight through to the death struggle so that he stood between the betjak and the tangle of arms and legs, and the flaying hand that held the knife. He stretched out his arm and pointed his brown finger at the knife, and then back at the over-turned betjak, and then at himself, and roared with raucous mirth. He looked ludicrous, fantastic, like an Asian Charlie Chaplin with his dancing arm waving above the fighters, and his hilarious, childlike laughter echoing itself in the hot dusty air. Horrified, with my eyes still on the struggling betjak-drivers, I felt my lips twitch. Near us, someone in the crowd giggled out loud.

Then a long, low rumble like distant thunder swelled that one giggle into a great growl of mass mirth.

The betjak driver who held the knife with fingers as thin and bony as the ribs under his arm, heard the rumble, and jumped like a panther to his feet. His eyes, blank with passion, fell for the first time on the little man, turned baffled to stare at the laughing mob, then switched back again. His adversary, as wary as an animal, crouched on his haunches and waited.

The hearty laugh of the little man rang out across the square, followed by his high shrill voice, convulsed with high-pitched irony.

"What are you – fighting about – you?" he demanded.

"Look at the other man's betjak! Your betjak is not hurt – his is upside down! Look at it! Look how funny it looks! And I was in it and now it's upside down. Not yours – his!"

He pointed his finger at the other betjak driver and slapped his thigh and roared again. The crowd roared with him and took up the chant:

"Not yours – his! Not yours – his! Not yours – his!"

It was like a Greek play with a chorus. On the stage outlined by our windscreen, not one of the three central characters moved, and their stillness was ominous. The man with the

knife, gripped pointed in his hand, was standing like a glow-
ering figure of wrath staring at the little buffoon, the unexpected clown, the purveyor of public ridicule, while his enemy
crouched behind him, alert and tense. Then the man with the
knife stepped forward one step, toward the little man and in-
stantly the chanting ceased. My hand flew to my throat. My
driver's hands closed tight on the steering wheel. The tense
crowd breathed as one and waited.

The little man did not give ground. Instead, he laughed
again, just once, like a crow, "Ha-ha," and then called out loud
and clear, "Me – look at me. I'm the one! Lucky me – the one
in the betjak that turned over. I'm the one that's supposed to
pay my fare for being turned over. Look at me – I am the one.
I am the one!"

Suddenly menacing, the crowd took up the chorus and
began to close in, chanting and shouting, feet pounding the
pavement in unison.

"Look at him – he is the one! Look at him – he is the one!"

I saw the betjak driver with the knife still in his hand turn to
run as the crowd surged forward with glee. At the same time, I
heard a police whistle somewhere across the other side of the
square. The crowd heard it too and affably cleared a pathway
for both the betjak-drivers. The one with the knife dropped his
weapon as he mounted his vehicle and pedalled away at top
speed without the encumbrance of his bewildered passenger,
who stood gawking in exactly the same place.

It is necessary to say here that this incident has taken longer
to write about than it will take to read; that it took even less
time to happen, to be lived through and, like agony, endured. In
Southeast Asia it takes no longer than five minutes for people
to swarm like ants and screech like locusts. As a foreigner you
sit rigid among them, terrified by sheer pressure, your heart
pounding, eyes and ears strained, helpless. In any large city it
takes at least this period of time for police to arrive, no matter

how vigilant, and just for the record I should add that police in Jakarta are not too numerous, comparatively speaking, and therefore a little prone to the hope that, if given a chance, the frequent traffic tangles may extricate themselves, even on Merdeka Square. The police whistle is always blown in advance and it is truly amazing how quickly a clumsy, excited mob can disperse. On this occasion the police arrived to demand an explanation just after the second betjak had been turned upright and wheeled away. The little man in the mussed white suit, sitting once again beside my driver, spoke to the police in rapid Bahasa for no more than a minute. The police laughed briefly and asked no further questions. We moved on as traffic cleared.

I reached forward and tapped the little man on the shoulder.

"Can I take you to a doctor," I asked him in my slow Bahasa, "or would you rather we took you home?"

"I would be grateful most to be taken home," he replied in equally slow English. "I must change my clothes." The small wrinkled face he turned toward me held an expression both shrewd and kind, "if you are not upset too much yourself, Nonja."

He shrugged but I could feel his weariness.

"The ignorant are stupid and violent, Nonja, but they laugh with equal ease – it is something you learn. The joke today is on me. The ladies of my household begged my car and, for the first time for many moons, I rode the betjak to go to the house of my brother, to borrow his car, which is not this day in use. It was, what you say in English, one thing follows the other." And he chuckled, only this time softly.

"Just the same, you might have been killed," I protested.

"It's not the good who die young, Nonja, or the bad. It's the serious, the serious, the for-themselves-too-serious people!"

And he turned in his seat and deliberately kept up a bird-like chuckling just loud enough to discourage further conversation and also, I suspected, as a suitable means of ignoring the pain of an ugly welt rising purple on his cheek, which would doubtless close his eye before the hour was out. Since he chose to ignore his bruising, I could scarcely mention a doctor again. My driver went to the door of his house with him and saw him safe inside. I had a feeling that in spite of his laughter he would remain indoors and respect the rest of his day of ill-omen in which one thing followed another.

"What a brave man," I said to my driver when he returned to the car.

The driver, who was one of the blessings of life in Jakarta, answered me slowly, in short clear phrases, which he knew I, with my limited knowledge of his language could comprehend. Since I no longer think of traffic in Jakarta without musing on the benefits of laughter, I will not forget the words he said.

"The day comes from heaven, Nonja, that brings a man with laughter bigger than fear."

GUIDO AND THE
GEDEH

To get to Djapanas it is necessary to drive through Bogor, where late starters from Jakarta can stop for lunch in the world-famous botanical gardens, the Kebun Raya, which lie under the conical shadow of the volcano called Salek.

Salek was one of the volcanoes on Guido's list, but not nearly as important as the Gedeh, which he would see every day from the hotel near Djapanas where he and his friends were going to spend the holiday. Guido was terribly excited to be getting close enough for a good look at the Gedeh, for this volcano had erupted within the last few years and he had written down the details in his special notebook. He knew, of course, that the Merapi in Central Java was bigger, and that Anak Krakatau – the island child that the great volcano Krakatau had thrown up from the sea in 1928 – were more interesting from a vulcanologist's point of view, particularly as Anak Krakatau had gone back into the sea, reappeared again and erupted as recently as 1950. But these volcanoes, like the parent Krakatau that had killed thirty thousand people when it blew up in 1883, were too tremendous for Guido to contemplate without trepidation and made him wish the certainty of his future profession as a vulcanologist had taken a little longer to germinate. Since Guido was so far only eleven years old, he thought about volcanoes like he thought about God.

Both were enormous, rumbling presences full of inexplicable power, fascinating and unpredictable. Both were fire in the bowels of the earth and thunder in the sky.

Surjo, Guido's Javanese friend who was sitting beside him in the car, thought God actually lived in volcanoes and that when people were bad and needed to be punished, the volcano erupted and drowned them in lava and ash that obliterated their house and rice-paddies. Guido tended to discount Surjo's theory, although it worried him a little. He had heard his parents say that some Indonesians were pagan animists, whatever that was, and full of superstitions that were divorced from true religion. But Surjo was a Christian who went to the same school as Guido, so that didn't hold. Nor, for that matter, had Guido had much satisfaction when he asked his father whether Vesuvius erupted on Pompei because of the wickedness of the Roman Empire of those days.

The information that Guido really preferred was the scientific kind that he could extract from his French friend Gerard, whose father was on intimate terms with a famous vulcanologist. Gerard's father, in contrast to his own, seemed to think that an interest in volcanoes showed the signs of an intelligence previously lacking in his son, and went out of his way to feed the new growth, quite unaware that Gerard's quick memory relayed the information for purposes of prestige to Guido, who was impressed enough to write down every word in his volcano notebook. On the last holiday to the hills from Jakarta, Guido had shared a room with Gerard, which gave plenty of opportunity to discuss volcanoes. But this time his mother and Gerard's had invited the new American boy, Buck Simpson, and his mother to share the holiday with them. Guido was pleased enough about this turn of events, for he liked Buck, who had fallen into place alongside Gerard and himself as the social and intellectual firsts at his level of the school strata, and he felt they made a splendid team along with Surjo, whose home-ground they shared. Buck was in no way the personal challenge to Guido that he was to Gerard, but his presence knocked out the promotion of conversations exclusive to volcanoes by the constant introduction of American technology. Guido had noticed, by Gerard's reaction, that this subject rated equally high in the estimation of Gerard's father, so he knew that on holiday volcano discussion would tend to peter out in favour of the height of the Empire State building. Under normal circumstances this did not matter too much, but for a holiday under the very shadow of the volcano Gedeh, Guido felt it necessary to fortify himself against New York and Detroit. He had asked his mother if he could invite Surjo as his guest.

Guido's mother agreed because, from her point of view, Surjo was a quiet, well-mannered boy and four boys seemed to her a more balanced responsibility than three boys when one of them was as volatile an influence on her son as Gerard. Besides, she was impressed with Guido's Christian generosity and kindness in wishing to ask his Indonesian friend. She had no idea, of course, that although Surjo was not as scientifically informed as Gerard about volcanoes, he provided a willing, if nervous, listener – providing the discussion swung round as it usually did to God. In a car, parents as well as children are forced to suffer the educational see-saw, and the first lesson on volcanoes was endured before the party driving to Djapanas reached the botanical gardens at Bogor.

"You see," Guido explained to Surjo by means of a little map in his notebook, "the volcano and earthquake belt is a kind of wide ribbon winding around the whole world underneath the mountains and the sea like a big dangerous snake. It goes up the coast of South and North America on the Pacific side, with a branch over Central America to the Atlantic Ocean where it goes under to come up again on the North African coast and under all the Mediterranean countries, which accounts for Vesuvius and Etna in my country like I told you. Then it goes down the East African coast, you know, Kilimanjaro and all that."

"Yes, you told me about that," Surjo said politely, hopefully looking out the window.

However, Guido felt it was very important that Surjo should be reminded of the whole volcano background before they came face to face with the Gedeh, so he continued the lesson with his finger on the map.

"That's only half, of course, Surjo. From the top of the West Coast of Canada, the belt crosses to Japan, where one arm goes around the North in a big circle that comes down through central Asia and Persia to follow the Himalayas and link up with the other arm going south, right through Java where we are. From here it skirts around the East Coast of Australia through New Zealand and down to Antarctica again. Anywhere in all those places where that belt is you can get an earthquake or eruption any old time!"

He stopped dramatically, out of breath momentarily, and then added, with awe in his voice, "It sure is something, isn't it?'

"It is a wonder of God," Surjo said.

"It's pretty special, don't you think, that you and I have always lived right on it, because it sure is the most wonderful phenomenon of nature. I'm glad I didn't get born on the East Coast of America or somewhere like that, aren't you?"

"I'm not sure. There's such a lot of volcanoes in Java it makes it very easy for God to punish our people. My mother told me that in 1947 a lot of volcanoes blew up and it was the Japanese and the Dutch who had been cruel during the war, and not the people who lived under the mountains. I can't understand why God did it."

"You can't question the wonders of God, and a volcano is a wonder of God. Your people must have done something if you believe God blew the volcano on purpose. I don't believe that, Surjo. The scientific books say the time just comes up and they go. It sure must have been something when Krakatau went up."

"I don't know about that, but my mother was in Bandung when the wrath of God blew up Gedeh where we're going. That was before she got to be a Christian."

"I wonder what makes them blow up every so often."

"I told you – people not being good, not looking after the poor and cheating in business."

"Why would God notice that?"

"God sees everything."

"I suppose so, but I don't think it has much to do with volcanoes, just the same, Surjo. But I'm going to find out. I'm going to be a vulcanologist."

"I'm not," Surjo said. "I don't like thinking about volcanoes. If I have to think about why Gedeh might blow up while we're there, I won't enjoy my holiday."

Guido's father was driving them up to Djapanas and had suffered just about enough snatches of his son's conversation, which he noticed his wife had begun to strain to hear.

"That will do, Guido," he said sharply in Italian, for he did not wish to embarrass his son in front of his guest.

"I won't have you spoil your mother's holiday with talk of volcanoes. If you must think about volcanoes then keep your thoughts to yourself, understand?"

"Yes, sir," Guido said promptly, not minding very much for they had almost arrived at the Kebun Raya.

When they got out of the car at the gate, Guido lagged a little behind the others, in order to get a good look at Mount Salek. A beggar came up beside him unobserved as he stared at the wisps of cotton-white cloud that wreathed the mountain like smoke.

"Saja rupiah, saja rupiah, one rupia," the beggar boy said.

Guido started. Then he looked down and was terribly shocked, so shocked that the colour flooded his neck and cheeks, and he ran like the wind to catch his parents and Surjo who were inside the gardens. The beggar was a boy his own age whose face came no higher than Guido's waist because he had no legs. Instead, what remained of his thighs rested on a small wooden platform on castor wheels so that he propelled himself by the palms of his hands flat on the road.

Breathless, Guido demanded of his parents and Surjo, "Did you see that boy? He's got no legs; no legs at all. How could God do that to anybody?"

They all turned, saw the boy at the gate, turned quickly and walked on.

"I don't think God did it, Guido," his father said, "much more likely a motor car. I'll give him something when we go out, poor boy."

"I will too," Surjo said. "I didn't see him coming in but he's often here. I always give him something. Most people in the new Indonesia don't but that one has to be a beggar."

The legless boy was at the gate when they returned to the car. Guido's father and Surjo each put a coin in his hand, but Guido lifted his eyes in the direction of the mountain and made straight for the car. He could not look at the beggar boy, so fiercely, so unreasonably handicapped, and he still felt God could have done something about it.

~

The hotel at Djapanas had a turquoise swimming pool and a beautiful garden. The air was sweet with the perfume of frangipani and jasmine. Pines and tree-fern shaded the mountain walks, and the red soil was so lush the palisade fences around the tiny Javanese houses and plantations sprouted in the sun. Beneath the long chain of the mountains capped by the ten thousand feet of the volcanic cone of the Gedeh, the foothill terrain was a landscape of prosperity and peace. The mothers of the boys sighed with relief and were anxious to rest after the heat and strain of Jakarta. The boys entertained themselves in the swimming pool and walked the nearer paths and roads – a freedom not permitted in the city. Part of every one of the first four days they sat in a bamboo copse a little distance behind the hotel back fence. They talked there, as boys always do in any sort of hide. Contrary to expectations, Guido had to admit that Buck had toned down his comparisons with the United States. He even seemed impressed with the height of the Gedeh and asked Surjo a lot of questions about the tea plantations, the teak forests, and whether he had ever seen quinine growing. Surjo was very pleased to have Buck's interest in his country, and Gerard brought up volcanoes again with revived respect as a method of keeping his proper place in the deliberations. In this good company, Guido felt able to air the sore spot in his mind that had refused to heal since he had seen the beggarboy with no legs in Bogor. Both Gerard and Buck had seen the boy on previous trips but not on this trip to Djapanas because Buck's mother had driven them up and, not being sure of the road, had refused to stop at Bogor or anywhere else. Gerard remarked that seeing that boy gave everybody the creeps so why talk about him, but Buck said it was a crime that the boy was not put in hospital and given artificial legs.

"I can't see how that would help him," Gerard said, with practical candour. "After all, how he is gets him a good living as a beggar. If he had artificial legs, he'd still be disabled but nobody would know it, so how would he eat?"

"The hospital would teach him how to make a living some other way, silly, or don't you have rehabilitation centres in France, either?"

"Sure we do, just as good as New York, too. But how would that help a boy with no legs in this country where they don't have them?"

"We do so have one," Surjo snapped.

"Then that boy ought to be in it," Buck said furiously.

"I bet you haven't got one with the best equipment at all. If you have, I'd sure like to see it. I bet my mum would, too. That boy's a disgrace and makes me sick at my stomach."

"I think there's only one," Surjo said miserably. "I think it is in Solo. That's a long way away from that boy and it costs a lot of money. My country isn't rich like yours."

"No, I guess not," Buck conceded.

Guido felt comforted by his friends but still terribly rebellious."I just can't see how God can allow such a cruel thing."

Gerard laughed at Guido, whose face was as long and doleful as a Modigliani."You never can, Guido. You never accept anything. It's like the volcanoes. You are always worrying about them. You can't help it that the boy has no legs. None of us can help it. Let's go and have a swim."

They got up and raced out of the bamboo copse.

~

On the morning of the fifth day of the holiday, Buck's mother asked the boys if there was anywhere they would like to go for a picnic, and Surjo said he thought since they were so close that they should see the Djibodas mountain garden, a nature reserve that was famous for its beauty and a wonderful place for a picnic. Buck's mother was delighted with the suggestion and went straight to get full driving directions from the hotel manager. Guido's mother said Djibodas was too near the volcano and was reluctant to go. Gerard's mother agreed with Guido's mother and felt equally nervous, but knew that active boys like Gerard could only be trusted for so long without some distraction and allowed herself to be persuaded. The hotel manager looked up at the sky, suspected the weather was wrong, but made no inhibitory remarks to Buck's mother because the policy was definitely to allow foreigners, particularly Americans, to do as they wished, on the assumption they would do it anyway. In this they were quite wrong, as Buck's mother was not in any way that kind of American, as either Guido's or Gerard's mother could have told them. As it was, lunches were ordered and they drove off in good faith, unoppressed by the sultry air and the low-clouded sky. Buck's mother sensed that the two European mothers sitting beside her in the front seat were less vivacious than usual but was undisturbed. Experience had taught her that mood temperatures rose and fell constantly among her continental contemporaries and were not to be taken personally. She had offered to take the boys herself if that was preferable. She had no suspicion that actual physical fear rode beside her in the car.

There was no fear in the back seat but there was keen and excited anticipation of adventure. Surjo topped excitement with pride that he should be able to display such a beautiful place to his American friend who had seen so much, and prayed gently to himself that the sun would come out to show off the gardens and the peak of the Gedeh. Buck was bursting with pride in his mother who really was super and game for anything. Gerard gained most of his excitement from the fact that he knew his and Guido's mothers were scared stiff to go so close to a volcano.

Guido's anticipation was entirely scientific. He was about to have his first close approach to a volcano. He knew that later on he would, of course, take part in aerial flights that allowed observation above the crater and ground expeditions that would take photographs and tabulate solfataric activity at dangerously close range. This small expedition was really of little importance except as a preliminary reconnoitre for his future work. Nevertheless, he felt constrained to make the most of it and sat with his volcano notebook in his hand. Surreptitiously he opened it at the page marked "Gedeh", which read:

'On November 20 in 1948 there was eruption and sound of falling rocks; on November 21 flashes at every few minutes seen at Tjibodas and rocks thrown out went until a distance of 800 metres; on November 23 at 7.00 hours, eruption clouds went into sky for 2,500 metres, rumblings were heard for 10 kilometres, blazes of fire were seen between eruptions, falling ashes went up to 50 kilometres away from volcano, half of the ash was magnetic, blue trembling hot gas escaped with the smoke.'

His eyes were glued to his own writing. Gosh, he hadn't taken it in before! Ashes went for fifty kilometres away from the volcano! No wonder Surjo was scared of volcanoes and thought God lived in them. They were driving right up close to Gedeh. Uncomfortably, Guido reached his hand behind his back and put the volcano notebook into the hip pocket of his shorts and glanced at his companions. The boys, the very best friends he had at the moment in the whole world, were sitting forward in their seats and laughing. Mrs Simpson, Buck's mother, was smoking a cigarette and putting the ash in the ashtray with a flick of her forefinger every two seconds. His own mama was sitting very still in the middle with her eyes fixed tightly ahead as if she was driving for Mrs Simpson. Mama didn't drive. Papa wouldn't let her because she was too nervous. Suddenly Guido felt very sorry for Mama. It was going to be terribly hard on Mama to have her only son take up such a dangerous occupation as vulcanology.

~

The sky was still heavily clouded when they reached the Kebun Tjibodas, the beautiful mountain garden. It was a working day and none of the usual crowds of sightseers were about. After an hour's wandering, the boys admitted they were hungry and the party went back to the car to get the picnic lunch. There were only four cars in the carpark and they ate close by under an enormous cedar that had spread its branches like a sweep of giant eagle wings over an emerald patch of grass. The mountain air was motionless, damply humid to the point of chilliness. There was about the place a sense of the mysterious silence of growth; rich, virulent growth that took its substance from the mountain. The foliage hung listless, strung taut on the breathing lianas. The trees were a canopy between the earth and the sky that grew through the unseen senses of sound, taste and smell, proliferous in shaded emerald abundance. Man did no more than trim and tend to allow himself the space to walk and the chance to learn his place in this creation. The garden belonged to the mountains and grew around its perimeter like a mystical skirt of mottled green.

From the carpark a path wound steeply up through natural vegetation to the highest possible view of the Gedeh. After lunch it was decided that only Ann Simpson should go with the boys to the top. The pressure of time for the return rested like a heavy cloak on the shoulders of the mothers. It had weighed down Guido's mother from the time of arrival and had communicated itself to Buck's mother who, being the driver, felt responsible. Gerard's mother preferred a second look at the flower displays to a long climb, and Guido's mother said they would be faster without her. All would meet at the car within an hour. The boys bounded up the hill like antelopes. Ann Simpson told them that if they went quietly, nature would reveal unexpected treasures of sight and sound. Buck and Surjo dropped back to keep her company. Guido kept a metre in front. He liked Buck's mother and was a little frightened he might break his resolve and tell the things he knew about Gedeh. Gerard rushed ahead – it was important to him to be first to the top.

The sun came out and filtered through the forest before they reached the outlook point that outlined the cone of Gedeh. The sky directly above the volcano was hard, brilliant blue, just for the moment of arrival. Surjo was overcome with joy that his friends should see the Gedeh in such beauty and cried out to Guido, who had halted ahead beside Gerard.

"It must be true. It is true, Guido, that God is in a volcano."

Ann Simpson smiled and put her arm on the shoulder of her son and her other arm on the shoulder of the Javanese boy.

"I am sure it is true, Surjo," she said, "that a volcano needs God to look after it."

But Guido did not answer because he was thinking of the hot burning ashes and the falling rocks and the eruption clouds that went straight up in the air for two and a half thousand metres. And as they stood watching the white wispy streamers of cloud gather momentum and change in front of their eyes with the rapidity of a chameleon from pearly grey to ominous black, Guido had a dreadful thought. It occurred to him that perhaps it was not God who was in volcanoes, but the Devil.

Ann Simpson said smartly, "Come along, boys. We must get down as fast as we can."

She did not like the look of the Gedeh wreathed in the mirror of smoke, even though she knew it was only darkening cloud. Under the suddenly dulled sky the mountain was no longer spectacular but malevolent, and the forest track beneath the struggling lianas menacing and eerie.

"I'll beat you down," Gerard yelled and was off down the path.

Buck and Surjo galloped after him, but Buck stopped and waited for his mother to catch up. That she was very pleased he had, he could tell by her face, and he was proud to have waited. He guessed she was suddenly tired and wondered why. She had seemed so bright when they reached the top.

"It won't take us any time to get down, Mum," he said. "We just gotta hop."

~

Guido decided to turn back to take just one last look at the Gedeh. After all, he was not likely to get another chance for a long time, and as he was collecting information about volcanoes, a look by himself for study purposes was warranted. He would run like the wind in just a minute to catch up with Mrs Simpson. But when he turned, he was amazed that his eyes saw nothing. Where the Gedeh had been was entirely cloud-covered like a distant bush fire. He stood still where he turned and squinted his eyes in amazement. You turned your back on the volcano and in one minute it was out of sight in a whirling puff of smoky vapour so that, to spite you, you couldn't see it anymore. It was mean! It wasn't God. It was the Devil!

A great rumble like the sound of a waterfall rose out of the Gedeh and the cloud shot up above it like driven steam. Then the steam dropped like a fog between Guido and Gedeh, and he knew the mountain was belching smoke, that the steam would rise and the ash fall. Fear gripped his throat so that his breath hissed out in a strangling whistle that should have been a scream.

It was a strange thing, but as he stood there petrified and speechless, the cloud cleared again and he saw the Gedeh out-lined against the sky with smoke circling the crater like the veil on the brim of a hat. Trembling in every pore of his skin, Guido knew the Devil was trying to erupt the Gedeh and that only God could stop it.

"Keep it in, God," he prayed. "Please keep it in and save us all. If you save me too, I'm going to grow up and be a vulcanologist and help save people from volcanoes. Don't let it kill us. I'd do anything if you'll keep it in. Keep it in!"

And Guido turned and started down the steep mountain path with his feet pounding like a drum: keep-it-in, keep-it-in, keep-it-in!

His feet beat the rhythm of the words in his head as the sky darkened and the rumble sounded again, and he remem-bered that the sun had only came out once and that it hadn't been a good day for a picnic but that he had persisted hard to come anyway. His mother hadn't wanted to come, and Gerard's mother hadn't wanted to come, and Buck and his mother had never been near a volcano before, and Surjo was trying to show off his country to please them all. He himself, Guido, was the one who studied volcanoes and he should have known God was giving a warning. There were only four cars in the park. Only four cars. That was good, really. It must be hard for God to get around to warn people. Like that boy without the legs. Maybe God tried but that day the boy wouldn't listen. God needed a lot of help. People were stubborn and selfish even about such dangerous things as volcanoes, and God had to look after over a hundred and fifty volcanoes in Indonesia alone. God needed a lot of help. God needed a lot of help!

He sobbed for breath as he stumbled, regained his tread, slipped and grabbed a swinging vine to steady himself against the fall. A bird flew straight down the path an inch above his head. He wondered then about the monkeys and the snakes and felt terribly lonely. His hopping rhythm re-established again; he prayed in gasps into the heavy oppressive air.

"Keep it in, God. Keep it in, God, until we get away. It's my fault. I'm the only one who knew about volcanoes. I'll help you look after the volcanoes when I grow up. I promise. I'll help that boy to get legs at that place Surjo knows about. I'll do that, too. I'll give my birthday money if you'll save us all. I'm nearly down, God. Keep it in until we get away. Keep it in!"

~

Gerard was the first to pound into the open from the mountain track. He raced across the grass towards the car screaming his excitement in French as his mother ran to meet him.

"Surjo says the volcano is going up. We'll have to get away as fast as we can."

His mother seized him and squeezed him, but he wriggled like an eel out of her embrace and stared in astonishment feeling her tears on his face. Embarrassed for his mother, he turned to Surjo who had caught up with them, but Surjo flew at his mother like a frightened bird and was hugged as he had been, and kissed on both cheeks. So Gerard knew the situation was beyond adventure and serious. When he saw the face of Guido's mother, fear hit him like a football in the stomach. Five minutes later, Ann Simpson and Buck ran across to the car but Guido was not with them. The haunted eyes of Guido's mother stared out of their sockets into Ann Simpson's white face.

"Guido, Guido? Where is my Guido?"

All of them stared in consternation at one another, three boys and three mothers, beside the only car left in the carpark underneath the rumbling volcano. Then Surjo put both his arms around Guido's mother and Buck stepped very close to Ann as she said she would go back immediately and look for Guido. But Gerard had already gone and was running like a streak of lightning across the grass while his mother screamed at him to come back and started to follow him towards the steep mountain path.

At this moment Guido came into view, running like a wobbly hare with a hound at his heels. Gerard gave an excited whoop and waited to turn and run in step beside him to the car. Both of them passed Gerard's mother and then Buck arrived breathless at the car door where Ann Simpson and Surjo had seated Guido's mother, who was nearly at the point of nervous collapse. Ann Simpson knew she could not wait for the reunion of mother and son to hear Guido's explanation and ordered the boys into the back seat of the car as quickly as they could and no nonsense. Guido was panting so hard he seemed temporarily helpless, so Buck pushed him in while Surjo ran round to get in the other side. Gerard stood with his mouth open waiting for his turn to scramble in when his mother came up behind him to administer a smack with such force she knocked him inside and adequately released the tension choked up inside herself. As she got into the car beside Guido's mother, Ann Simpson started the engine and they were off.

From somewhere inside its melting rock, the Gedeh groaned again like distant thunder.

"Close all your windows," Ann Simpson ordered, thinking of ash, "and sit still in the back."

Gerard saw his mother put her arm around Guido's mother to keep her steady and rubbed his stinging ear with surprise but no rancour. Surjo closed his eyes. Very quietly, with his gaze on the back of his mother's head, Buck passed out life-savers one by one to each boy, and then hesitated about slipping the package to Gerard's mother. Guido, because he sensed his mother was prostrated decided to make his speech before he ate his lifesaver, even though his throat was dry.

"Mama," he croaked, "listen, Mama. You don't have to be frightened. We'll be safe. I've promised to help God with volcanoes when I grow up, and in the meantime I'm going to help that boy at Bogor get new legs. I've promised all my birthday money, Mama."

"Why?" Gerard demanded, being the only one capable of speech.

"So God would keep the eruption in until we get back to the hotel."

"Gee!" Buck exploded.

Ann Simpson, with her eyes steady on the road and her foot hard on the accelerator, gripped the wheel tighter as the corner of her mouth twitched. She was conscious that Gerard's mother had reached for a cigarette and felt Guido's mother straighten a little in the seat beside her.

"Buck," she said lightly, "I think I will have one of those life-savers of yours, if you can put it in my mouth – not that any of us really need a lifesaver with Guido to look after us. I think you must feel very proud of Guido, Maria. I do."

"Gee, me too," Buck said. "Can I put some money in too, Mum?"

"Alors!" Gerard muttered. "I haven't got much. I've spent my allowance, but I bet I can earn some. Can I, Maman?"

His mother smiled. "Oui, you can earn some, Gerard. I will give you an advance – but for you it will be difficult to earn, mon fils, for we must keep it a secret, n'est pas, about Guido and God and the Gedeh. You understand?"

~

It was a long, hot, subdued drive back to the hotel, and the aftermath of unspeakable excitement ached in their cramped bones as they drew near the driveway where a crowd awaited them anxiously with field-glasses trained on the Gedeh puffing smoke into the evening sky. The manager had been severely criticised for letting them go, and a reporter stood by with his eye on the stairs that led to the telephone.

"Don't move, boys," Ann Simpson said, forestalling their exit from the car.

"I'm going to drive right up so we can go in the back way to our rooms to wash. We've had a wonderful picnic and we don't want to spoil it."

And when the manager stopped her at the open gate, she put her head out the window with her hair all wind-blown and ignored his excited face.

"We started back as soon as we could after we heard the first rumble. Is everything OK here?"

It was terribly hard on Gerard, who learned in that understatement just how he was expected to earn his share of a safe return from the Gedeh. But harder for Guido, who had to support his mother into her room, alone with her for the first time after the longest silence she had ever made him endure. But he felt sad for his mother, more than for himself, because he knew he had grown up somehow and had taken the first step in coming to terms with his destiny. The surprising thing was that his mother had accepted his destiny and seem relieved, for all she said was, "Why, Guido, out of all the sciences do you have to choose volcanoes? Mama Mia, how am I going to stand it?"

THE FIFTH PILLAR

As usual, Sumekto started his day violently, just before daylight, awakened by Uncle Surio pounding his shoulder. The whole of Sumekto's small frame reacted with the energy of a pricked insect trying to wriggle back to the broken cocoon of previous security. In his dream he invariably managed to dispose of his uncle and live in a garden but awake he could never tell whether the dream made his uncle dead or whether he himself had mustered up the courage to run away.

Walking beside his aunt, who was pregnant again, Sumekto carried the baby as far as the road junction near the marketplace. There the family divided. His aunt took the baby and the hand of the next smallest child and proceeded to Bandung where she had work washing clothes. The eldest girl, Widi, took her two brothers and went to sleep in the schoolground until the 8 a.m. classes. Uncle Surio sat down with Sumekto under a sugar-palm where he gave the boy a small cloth full of miscellanea to sell: a comb, pins, a bit of elastic, pencils. Sumekto knew his uncle did not trust him, for there were other things in his uncle's bundle like cigarettes, ball pens, silver brooches and rings, even food. Uncle Surio wanted Sumekto hungry enough to force himself back for a meal so that after he ate, he could be sent out to sell again.

Sumekto watched his uncle walk away and grew happy because he had evolved a scheme to deceive his uncle and still have the one rupiah expected from his sales. When people

69

bought from Sumekto it was because he looked hungry and had the soft eyes and docile manner of a gazelle. This kind of purchaser took one or two articles and gave him the whole rupiah. One day, a lady with pleats in her skirt had given him all the change in her purse for one pencil. After that, Sumekto had woven a flat envelope out of dead bamboo fronds to hide in a place of bamboo peelings. As soon as his uncle was out of sight, he went to his cache to see if everything was safe. Only once had he decided to take out a rupiah and cache away the new goods to sell the next day and, by this means, gain the wonderful time for sleep before school that he so much envied his cousins – but the plan had miscarried. As he could not risk being seen asleep near the school, he had been obliged to find a spot too far away for the school-bell to wake him and had slept until noon and had only just managed to arrive at the school ground before his cousin Widi missed him. Fortunately, Widi was not in the same class as Sumekto, being a little older and very much smarter – so smart, in fact, that it was because of her progress that he and the little brothers had got into school at all. Sumekto did not blame Widi for reporting his slightest misdemeanour to her father – it shifted responsibility away from herself and she had to use any means to stay at school as long as she could. He appreciated that she did not lie about him unless her shoulders were squeezed, and she had helped him with the reading and writing so that now he did not forget everything that he had learned on the days when he was tired; but he was frightened to try to sleep any more in the daytime.

He hoped very hard that he would see the special lady to-day, for she always bought from him. Every time she did, he made a little profit and had the extra rupiah to give to his uncle when he was sent out at night. All he really had to do then was walk as far as his cache and wander around a while in the safe places, even if he did not sell anything. Having been set upon once after dark, he had grown cunning. There were times, like last night, when he wished he could explain how cunning he was to his aunt – but he did not dare. Any more than he dared lie down to rest away from home during his evening session in case he did not wake up until morning.

Sumekto yawned as he replaced his cache and made his way in the beauty of the early morning to the place at the nearest point to the market where the people came to bathe and make a daily toilet in the same canal already used further up in his own desa. He usually stood in this place, near and yet not too close to the food-sellers. Sometimes he sold something to a betjak driver here, and it was still much too early to expect the lady who could not resist his eyes. He felt so tired he knew he must not sit down, and his mind kept wandering back to his dream that he could not quite recall. It had been a very special dream and it hovered as close as a tantalising butterfly.

After an hour and a half, a betjak driver nearly knocked Sumekto down so he knew he must have been dozing on his feet. He had sold nothing. Shaking himself, he went to stand where the lady usually came by and waited until it was seven-thirty by the sun. She did not come. Then he wandered back to his cache, hid away his goods and counted his cents to make sure he had almost a rupiah to give his uncle in case the afternoon was as bad as the morning. By eight o'clock, he was happily waiting in line to enter school, his head up, his narrow shoulders squared. He was one of the elect who had some-how been chosen to receive an education; a member of the community that would one day be literate.

~

The first half hour of school was weekly assembly for the recitation of the Pancasila, after which the head teacher ex-plained the five principles and what each image stood for on the shield. First, belief in God, for everyone the freedom of their own religion – this was the Star in the centre of the national emblem; second, Nationalism, the unit of the whole people symbolised on the Shield by the spreading and rooting branches of the Banyan Tree; third, the picture of the linked chain that meant Humanitarianism making one big family of all nations and races; fourth, Democracy, the strong, hard Bull's Head of government by consent of all the people; and the great and final fifth – Social, of growing cotton to show that there would be enough food and clothing for everybody to live in prosperity in the new Indonesia. A tremendous pride swelled Sumekto's heart, for when he heard the explanation of the fifth principle, he recognised the picture in his dream.

Back in the classroom after the shuffle into seats, there was a sudden hush as the head of every child bent forward over an exercise book and the teacher began to write on the black-board the words they were to copy. While Sumekto formed the letters, he mused on the wonderful message that made him part of a free country of opportunity where, because of the fifth great pillar, there would be no hunger and a doctor to look after everybody like his aunt who was always sick. There would be clothing for everyone, and each family would have a house exactly the same as the one he saw in his dream, where a boy walked into his own garden and picked a mango and a banana for his breakfast after waking up to the sweet smell of jasmine above his windowsill. Just like in his dream, each child would have a mother with pleats in her sarong and would run straight home from school to be warmed by her loving smile. Every boy would have a strong, smiling father who earned the rice and cotton and then took a ball-point pen to correct a mistake his son made trying to spell. Their house would be on a beautiful open country road where no thieves lurked to take away the wealth the people carried, and all families would stop happily in the market to buy food from the tukangs, and even balloons and books for the children to take to school to show the teacher. He had seen it all in his dream, every bit of it, and now he knew it was true for he had heard it in school. He could hear the laughter of it bubbling up around him like a blessing.

It seemed strange, at first, that the hand on his shoulder was not his uncle's and that the shaking of his shoulder was gentle, but the laughter was real. The high, shrill laughter of the other children flowed into his consciousness like the early morning chatter of mynah birds. The moment of his waking was terrible, and he denied it with his head still on his arms on the desk as long as he could, until the flush of shame flowed away with the dream and he could lift his face and smile inanely like poor, mad Sugila in the market.

His teacher was very young and new to the village. Just graduated from the training school in Jakarta, she knew she had to be strict on behalf of education in the new Indonesia. She reprimanded the children sharply for their laughter.

"Sumekto is tired," she said. "He may have been up all night. That is why he fell asleep."

"Sumekto has been up all night," the children chorused. "That is why he fell asleep."

"Were you sick in the night, Sumekto?" the teacher asked.

"No." Sumekto lied. "I slept in my bed and woke up to the smell of jasmine coming in the window." His voice was sharp and insolent with the embarrassment of the words, which came straight out of the dream.

The teacher drew in her breath and tensed her shoulders. She was unsure about this Sumekto who so often gazed without comprehension at the blackboard beyond her head, instead of at her face; whose eyes were dark with the promise of wisdom while his brain seemed incapable of grasping the day-to-day addition of facts required for the simplest progress. He learned in jerks of concentration from time to time, in spasms of forced effort beyond the capacity of any other child in the class, but usually he was dull beyond her power of stimulation.

Even his impertinence seemed too distant for normal reprimand.

"I think we will ask your father to come for a talk, Sumekto," she said.

Sumekto stood up.

"He hasn't got a father," the children chorused again. "He lives with his Uncle Surio who is Widi's father."

A baffled resentment rose in the teacher, more for herself than Sumekto.

"Very well, children," she snapped, "back to work. Perhaps we will have a talk to Sumekto's uncle then."

She walked straight up to the blackboard and all the pupils bent over their books because they knew their teacher was angry. Sumekto knew she was angry too, so nothing mattered any more. The dream was shattered. He ran straight out the door, down the hall and out into the school grounds. He kept running right through the market street and further than that down the road to his cache. He went in behind the bamboo and lay down.

~

For a little while, Sumekto let the tears squeeze out of his eyes. He realised he was too big a boy to cry like a baby and had managed for almost a year to freeze the tears that gathered behind his eyes when his uncle beat him. Women wept and girls like Widi sniffled out of fear, but once he had seen a man cry at a funeral. Sumekto had been impressed because a funeral was a common occurrence in any kampong. Now, for the first time, he understood why death alone made excuse for even a man to weep. The tears were not for yourself but for something you would never see again, for the farewell of a closed face. It did not have to be a human face; it could be the face of a dream that had to be put away and forgotten. A boy had to live, and life would not let him sleep all the time to enjoy a dream that was dead. Even so, Sumekto was only a little boy, so after a while his swollen eyes closed and he slept.

When he woke, it was dark, and in spite of the chill and a gnawing hunger, he felt strangely relieved and refreshed. He put his hand into the bamboo to retrieve the woven package from his cache so he could decide what to do. Many walk the roads of Java and where poverty stalks with them as close as a shadow, even a small boy's treasure is worth investigating as possible alleviation of the daily need.

The packet was not there.

Sumekto sat very still after his futile search. This time he shed no tears. His mind was clear and bright after his long sleep, and he sensed that exhaustion and inexperience had made him careless of his cunning. He remembered exactly what had been in the packet; perhaps enough small change to make three-quarters of a rupiah, a few small articles worth altogether no more than two rupiahs in the shops, a small stub of pencil and a few scraps of paper covered with a small boy's letters and numbers. Hope was not in the packet, nor return to school nor the dream. It contained no more than the promise of a daily meal, earned with blows and recriminations, and the thought came immediately to Sumekto that his uncle had stolen the goods to sell as well as all the cigarettes and brooches and rings, so therefore he, Sumekto, could as easily beg or steal enough to eat. It would not matter now, since the chance was lost to be one of the elect in the future community of the literate.

A shiver ran up Sumekto's spine, for the night air was cold at the edge of the hills. It would be much warmer in the humid capital city of Jakarta for a boy without a kain to wrap around his shoulders. To escape his uncle, he could go to the great city by the back roads. He knew how to start by following the stream that would provide water and led, after only one kilometre, through banana and paw-paw plantations where he could steal food.

He stood up, peered curiously both ways along the road, and listened intently to catch the direction of distant voices in the marketplace. Then he set out for Jakarta where, after all, he would merely add one more to a population of nine million and find it unexpectedly easy to lose an identity so precariously established.

PLAY OF SHADOWS

The house was set well back and in the shade of many trees and the perfume of budding cloves and the sweet scent of the blossoming djeruk filtered in through the open door to mingle with the warm smell of wax and leather. Despite the protection of the trees, the bamboo blinds were lowered against the heat and the room was sombre as the flickering sunlight fell on the carved heads and disclosed the shadowed wooden arms and faces of the puppets hung upon the walls. It was a magnificent display of the exotic legend of India created in the living art of Indonesia. All was broken shadow, purple-brown patches of shadow-play; a study of Wayang – fascinating, inscrutable.

Gratefully, I turned to Jan Strato, who was a specialist in Wayang and who had offered to show me the puppets of his collection when I visited Jogja.

"How fascinating they are," I said. "You know, I remember seeing one or two like these at the Jakarta airport when flying home from London years ago, and I have been furious with myself ever since for not buying them."

"I can understand that. For me the first fascination was the same, in fact, as you see, it became an obsession with me. But now I am here in Java I see so many I do not know how to choose."

"Do you buy only this kind?" I asked.

"Yes, only this kind with the carved wooden heads, beautifully and elaborately painted. See how the arms are jointed at the shoulder, the elbow, and the wrist, and notice how this solid head can bow, turn, and twist. During a performance late at night in the shadowed light of two hanging lamps, these puppets in their beautiful costumes become, in the hands of a master, alive and real – creatures of the inner world of the spirit of man, the living embodiment of good and evil. Would you like to sit in the garden for a cool drink while I tell you about the Wayang?"

"Indeed, I would. But first, if you don't mind, I would like to look at one of your puppets again."

"You already have a favourite?"

"Yes, this one. It is so beautiful and yet it has all the sadness of a dying aristocracy in the expression of the face; or perhaps carved in the long, elegant and useless fingers of the hands. Somehow it looks as if it has never been allowed to participate in a shadow-play, has never even been manipulated."

Jan Strato laughed. "I am sorry Susi is away," he said. "She would have liked to meet you. If she has a favourite – which, mind you, she will never admit – it is this one you admire. Come, we will sit in the garden."

So, we sat outside at a small table and a servant brought us glasses of sweet orange to drink while I heard the ancient Hindu legend of the Pendawa that represented the good, and their rivals Kurawa that stood for evil, and how they battled; and how Prince Arjuna was the hero of the good and triumphed again and again over the cunning forces of evil that waited to waylay him at every point of his journey.

"The highlight of the midnight show is always three clowns who are the servants of Arjuna," Jan said.

"There are always three big fights to be won by the Pendawas and the three faithful men-servants who seem to identify with the ordinary village people are hilariously funny and manage to save the prince despite buffoonery and homespun tactics. These are the ugly puppets, the useful outsiders, the caricatures. You see within the art the puppets have a pre-scribed facial form for the good and the bad characters. You will have noticed that Arjuna is always handsome and white. But within this restriction the creative variety is amazing. Mind you, this is also true of the clowns." He paused, and then re-peated because he had touched a memory, "in fact, if you are not wise enough, it can be too true of the clowns."

"Have you been collecting puppets for a long time, Jan?" I asked.

"Ever since the war ended and we came back to Java."

"But you do not have any clowns as you call them?"

"No. I only collect the Pendawa. A collector must limit his choice for specialisation."He stopped and chuckled, settled back in his chair and took his pipe from his pocket."Besides, my wife will not allow a clown in the house."

There is always a moment before a story begins when you sit silent and wait. Jan lit his pipe, and I breathed in the aroma of the spice trees and the citrus.

"From the first moment I saw the puppets," Jan began, "I couldn't be kept away from the shadow-play. I was also not long married and very happy despite the difficult times. Java, to Susi and me, was like a childhood fantasy re-lived, for we had both been sent home to school well before the war and lived out its miseries in Europe instead of the East. After we met and married, we came out here like a couple returning to a haunting dream. My job as an accountant with a firm of tea exporters in Jakarta included a little house to rent, which suited us very well. Strange as it may seem to you, we believed in Indonesian independence and concentrated on speaking Bahasa as well as our neighbours. My hobby from the begin-ning was the Wayang shadow-play, and after we worked out our living budget, which was no easy task in those days, we hunted the curio shops and country markets for inexpensive puppets of the kind I liked with wooden rather than kulit, that is to say, leather heads. We managed, I think, only about half a dozen in the first three years, certainly no more. These decorated a wall of our small sitting room, which Susi arranged with rattan chairs, batik cushions and, of course, a little carved teak table to suit them.

On behalf of my firm, I had to travel around to the tea plantations from time to time. On one of those trips, I brought Susi here to Jogja with me for a week's holiday, left her to amuse herself while I went out daily to one of the plantations to straighten the accounts. Susi wandered around the town, which she loved, and poked into all sorts of little shops and markets. When we packed up to go home, one of her bags was heavy with a surprise for my Saint's Day. She had found, of all things, a clown puppet, and somehow saved the money to buy it.

I wish you could have seen that puppet as I saw it on the day it was presented to me. I was appalled at its ugliness. I knew Susi could not have had much money, but I felt that whatever she had spent on it was wasted. It was not even a 'beautiful ugly' but atrocious; roughly gouged rather than carved and daubed with paint like a caricature. Worst of all, the wooden head was as heavy as iron and strangely unbalanced like a bird with a stiff neck. Only its dress was good: a kain of royal design on bark cloth. I felt dreadful about that puppet. Susi was proud of her unusual choice and had hoped that I would find it fun. It was so original, she said, so different, and probably had some history of interest – although the ignorant tukang who sold it to her in the market could tell her nothing of its origin. My disappointment was so acute I felt the tukang was ashamed to say his toothless grandmother had battered the thing into being, but I managed to hold my tongue, realising that already I was becoming a snob about my puppets, fancying myself as a connoisseur and a critic of the art of Wayang.

We had difficulty hanging the new puppet. Twice it fell to the floor with a thump that almost dislodged the hooks that supported the others. Eventually, we fixed it on a small frame of bamboo, higher on the wall and a little apart. Placed like this, with its arms secured to take the weight of the angled head, I had to admit the puppet assumed a character unnoticed when it was held in the hand. The painted eyes, unevenly outlined with an atrocious sweep of uncontrolled black caught all the lights and shadows, making the clown interesting as sinister, if not humorous as intended. I sighed with relief, for the hung puppet did not look so crude and belied my fear that it would mar the appearance of my collection.

But Susi, who had thought it no more than an amusing oddity, was overcome to see the crooked head take shadow life on the wall.

'I don't think it is a Pendawa clown at all,' she said nervously. 'I think it is a tricky Kurawa. Do you think it might be unlucky?'

'Not at all,' I cried grandly out of my relief. 'How could a gift you found all by yourself for my Saint's Day be unlucky? What does it matter if it is a Kurawa? How could there be a shadow-play at all if there was no Kurawa for the Pendawa to defeat? There must be evil to contrast the good. I like it there on its own side of the wall.'

Susi, I may say, is a beautiful woman, but for all that has always been highly sensitive and shy. In those days she made me feel a great protecting hero for no other purpose than the preservation of her fair loveliness. I remember I took her in my arms and kissed her until she laughed and ran away to stand under the puppet grimacing down at us from the decorative wall.

'You do like it,' she announced happily. 'I didn't think you did at first. So, I will like it too, even if it is a Kurawa.'

Our life moved forward contentedly, but not long after we had to give up our journeys to the villages, sitting up all night looking at the Wayang Kulit, for Susi was expecting our first child and was forced to conserve her strength for a hospital stay. She was a frail little thing whose pregnancy came hard. At just this time, I was promoted to manage my firm's branch here in Jogja, and our doctor suggested that the move would be too much for Susi and asked if I could afford to send her home to Europe to have the baby. I did not hesitate for a moment. What was best for Susi was best for me. I would be lonely, but she would have the specialised care she needed. While she was away, I would establish myself in Jogja and make a wonderful new home to welcome her back. It was all arranged, and Susi prepared to depart by sea in a month's time. It was a difficult month. We had never been parted before and Susi wanted both to have the baby in Amsterdam and make the move with me to Jogja. She grew so nervous she thought she was being followed and would not leave the house alone, even to go to the market. She insisted on packing up all our china herself, and persuaded me to take down the puppets from the wall so she could wrap them carefully in tissue paper and put them in a trunk ready for the move. Even before she left, our little house seemed barren and empty. Susi had four months to wait for the arrival of the baby. I had three months before the move to Jogja. The day after Susi sailed, I put all the packed-up boxes and trunks into store, moved out of the lonely little house and took a cheap room in the city. Whenever I could, I went by myself or with Indonesian friends to some performance of the Wayang, but I collected no more puppets until I was established here in my comfortable manager's house with our beautiful view of the heavily forested mountain slopes. As you see, the house is set in an atmosphere of serenity, and I felt so proud to be able to offer it to Susi when she returned with our son. Before I went to Jakarta to meet her ship, I furnished the house with some carved teak furniture sold by a Dutch family retiring to Holland. I also increased my collection of wooden-headed puppets by three, but I waited for Susi to arrange them on the wall with the others, which were waiting in the trunk recently delivered from Jakarta for her homecoming. For the rest, everything was in order for her arrival, and I left the house under the expert care of my newly acquired houseboy, a funny little fellow called Tiap who, for over a month, had been attending to my bachelor needs with the kind of unobtrusive precision I hoped would please Susi and relieve her of all worry except for the care of the child. She would, of course, take her time to find a suitable babu she could trust, and then I felt would settle into her new home with complete contentment. So much for the dreams of men!

Susi looked wonderful on her return, her skin fresh and delicate as porcelain, her heavy, fair hair shining with life, her soft doe-eyes glowing with love and pride. The baby was a big fellow for the tender number of his days, and had been a great attraction on the voyage. He and Susi had been very spoiled by passengers and crew, and it seemed to me that all the painful shyness of Susi had been dissipated by her motherhood. My pride as husband and father glowed like a fire in my chest as I thought that I had provided in Jogja the perfect setting for this regal pair.

Except for one unexpected flaw, the setting really was perfect for Susi. As I expected, she loved the house as much as I did, adored the view, and congratulated me on the purchase of the teak furniture. She was thrilled that I had left the arrangement of the puppets and other personal pieces until her return. She said the climate of Jogja was far superior to that of Jakarta and that she felt in her bones that she and the baby would thrive in it. Her delight in the carefully scrubbed tile floors and the neat, hygienic kitchen was obvious. Her first luncheon at the teak dining table was delicious and meticulously set and served. But whenever Tiap came into a room, she froze.

Now, there was nothing exceptional about Tiap beyond his efficiency, which could not be denied, and perhaps the long, thin fingers of his unwrinkled hands as he executed his duties. Without doubt, he was one of those rare servants found only on occasion by even the most fortunate employers in Indonesia. I paid him only the minimum average wage, which he seemed happy to accept, although it was evident that his apprenticeship had been served in richer homes than mine. Susi knew this immediately.

'Where did you find Tiap?' she asked the first night in the privacy of our bedroom. 'Did you bring him with you from Jakarta?'

'Jakarta?' I queried, astonished. 'Have you forgotten I wrote you that he turned up here at the house about a week after I took it over and asked if I needed a houseboy? He's a local man, says he was born in a desa about ten kilometres from Jogja.'

'You didn't think it was strange that he just turned up like that, asking for a job?'

'No, why should I? You know what the grapevine is. The boy who did my shirts at the hotel may have told him, or the neighbours, anybody.'

'And when he came, you just took him, or did you choose him from among others?'

I began to feel a measure of her agitation. 'Look, Susi,' I said, 'if he doesn't suit you, you can change later after you get settled in. I just wanted everything as comfortable as possible for your arrival.'

'Oh, my dear,' she said. 'I know that, and I'm delighted with everything you've done, and from what I can see, Tiap is a wonderful houseboy. I was only curious about him, about his references.'

'That's why I took him – I couldn't fault his references. There didn't seem to be any need to interview anybody else.'

'Were his references from Jakarta?'

'No, Susi. He did not have one reference from Jakarta. His references were from right here in Jogja. His last employers returned to Rotterdam two months ago.'

'I see. Oh, well...'

'Oh, well, what?'

'Nothing important, it was just that I thought I had seen him in Jakarta, that's all, working for one of our friends or something like that. It really doesn't matter, and if he really is as good as he seems to be, you certainly need not worry that I will let him go, unless, of course, he can't get on with Babu or something as drastic as that.'

There was, of course, nothing as drastic as that. The new babu and Tiap respected one another and mutually adored the baby. The household ran like clockwork. I have never been so fortunate as to enjoy such service since.

Susi helped me arrange the collection of puppets on the wall, the ugly duckling taking a place among them with an expression of sardonic glee. I anchored it well in a new, specially constructed head support that straightened the neck. Tiap attended the collection with careful, gentle pride and the daily use of a feather duster. Susi, as was natural, I thought, devoted all her interest to the baby and left the study of Wayang lore and puppets to me. I talked to her at length about the discoveries I had made during her absence in my reading on the subject. Always she listened to me politely, but I had a feeling her heart no longer lay with the collection of puppets. In the evening after dinner, taking our coffee together, I sat where her eyes fell only on a bowl of flowers and me.

One day, when our son was six months old, I came home early to tell Susi I would have to take a trip out to one of the plantations and would be away for about five days. I found Susi sitting in a little dressing room off our bedroom, which she had converted into a nursery. The baby was asleep, but Susi was reading peacefully, like a monk in a retreat, in an armchair placed between a carefully arranged table and a bookcase. The corner had a well-used look, and I knew immediately that as soon as the babu went off-duty when I returned to work after lunch, Susi settled into this place in preference to any other room in the house, even the lovely living room with the view of the mountains, the teak furniture, and the puppets. For some reason it gave me a very odd feeling to make this discovery, in fact, so peculiar was my reaction, I felt it better, at least for the time being, not to speak of it. In order not to wake the baby, Susi put her finger to her lips and without speech, backed me out of the room and followed me to the bedroom, closing the door softly behind her. Then she spoke, and her words were a flat, blank and unemotional statement, obviously rehearsed against the inevitable time when I would discover her hide and expect an explanation of it.

'Little Jan looked flushed, so I decided to sit with him while Babu is away.' Then she added, with an equally determined lightness: 'Whatever brings you home at this early hour? No work?'

'Too much work,' I replied, perhaps a little sharply. 'Shall we go to the living room where we don't have to whisper?'

'If you wish,' she agreed, 'although it seems a shame to disturb Tiap, who always has his afternoon sleep outside the living room windows.'

'For heaven's sake, why don't you tell him to sleep some-where else if you don't want him there?'

'I did, then he slept under the tree at the front fence, but still in front of the window. I really can't be bothered to ask him to move again, Jan.'

'If you don't want him sleeping in the front garden, then I'll tell him.'

'No, Jan, please don't tell him on my account. You will only upset him, and it is hardly worth it. He only thinks he is guarding your collection of puppets when no-one is about in the afternoon.'

'Guarding the puppets? You must be joking, Susi. Did he tell you that when you asked him to move?'

'Oh, no; if I had known I would not have asked him. It made so little difference anyway for he just gradually moved back a little closer to the window every day.'

Her voice seemed stressed, I noticed, although deliberately matter of fact, and I remembered that the night before she had seemed very tired and had taken herself off to bed right after coffee. Surely she was not dwelling on this idea of hers that Tiap was guarding the puppets? She had shown so little interest in the puppets lately. Perhaps I glanced at her apprehensively because she suddenly laughed.

'You look so serious all of a sudden, Jan,' she said. 'Almost angry. Come and have a drink. I'll call Tiap to get it for us. And please, don't worry. I don't mind in the least that Tiap has taken such a notion to your puppets and wants to take special care of them. He looks after them beautifully and that suits me, for I really don't have time for them now with the baby.'

Now, Susi had plenty of time and the baby was as healthy as a well-fed kitten. We were, at that time, only becoming acquainted with our neighbours and colleagues, so even her social obligations were not heavy, and she had no household worries whatsoever. I watched her go out into the hall toward the kitchen to hit the big gong we used to summon Tiap. Then something made me turn and stealthily open the door to the nursery where my son slept to look at the book she had been reading. It was an old parchment-coloured pamphlet I had forgotten I had, written by a Dutchman in 1896 entitled Royal Wayang Puppetry in Solo and Jogjakarta.

There was nothing I could do but sneak out the door again, walk into the living room and take my usual seat facing the wall of puppets. The ugly clown leered at me as the hot, saturated air of mid-afternoon broke out in a sweat on my forehead and soaked the shirt on my back. Susi looked very cool and composed in pale blue linen as she took her seat on the other side of the table and waited for Tiap to bring in the drinks on a tray. Tiap bowed and smiled but was in no way surprised to see me, having, I surmised suspiciously, already watched me walk in the gate without rising from his chosen place of siesta. He was very small in his white coat and brown-patterned head gear. Except for the white coat, all of him was as brown and unspectacular as a block of wood. Even the eyelids that wrinkled over his black eyes were the colour of brown paper. He could have been a mechanical wooden puppet himself, I reflected, except for the breath of life.

'Do you like the Wayang Kulit?' I demanded of him suddenly as he handed me a glass of ale. Out of the corner of my eye I saw Susi stiffen.

'I am Javanese,' Tiap said. 'It is the art of my life and the life of my ancestors, Tuan.'

'You look after my puppet collection very well, I notice. Do you think I have chosen wisely?'

'Your taste is in the spirit of the Wayang, Tuan.'

'Do you have a favourite, Tiap?'

The thin parchment lids lowered over his eyes.

'Not as yet, Tuan.'

Susi waited no longer than the time it took for Tiap to leave the room. 'I will go and get the baby,' she informed me, brightly rising to her feet.

'It is time for him to wake up and he loves to be with you. When we come back you can tell me what brought you home so early.'

But by the time she returned with the baby in her arms, I had nothing to tell her as I had decided to send my Chinese assistant out to the tea plantation instead of making the trip myself."

~

"Four days later the West Monsoon broke earlier than expected and the rain fell in torrents after a thunderstorm of such violence that Susi and I awoke in the night under the impression that the roof was collapsing on top of our heads. Lightning flashed in rocket streaks at the windows, and the branches of the trees in the garden were whipped into turmoil like the waves of the sea. The house literally wheezed as I sat up in bed to put on the light for Susi, who rushed to get the baby. The power, which was not good at the best of times, had failed completely, so I began to search for the flashlight, which led me, still confused by sleep, from one drawer in the bedroom to another, until I was suddenly awakened by a closer clap of thunder and remembered I had left it in the teak desk just inside the living room door. I helped Susi push the baby's cot into place beside our bed, put her safely beside it, checked the shutters at the window and went for the flashlight.

Exactly as I arrived at the living room door there was a scintillating flash of lightning. A dark form, prostrated headfirst toward the wall that displayed my puppets, was momentarily illuminated in the glow. Startled, I stepped back involuntarily against the wall of the hall, like a thief hiding in my own house. I waited to recover my breath and held it long enough for my mind to clear and circle with common-sense the sudden unexpected and unmasculine clutch of fear. Naturally, as I breathed again, I thought I had suffered an hallucination, had seen a shadow forced into shape by the lightning. The thing to do was wait and make better use of the next flash, which would prove me right or wrong. I turned to put myself in position and found I had no need for lightning. The distant flashing that preceded the rumbling thunder was light enough, as my eyes had grown accustomed to the dark. Deliberately, rhythmically, the shadowy form on my floor rose to its knees, prostrated itself, lifted its head and arms, prostrated again. There could be no doubt that it was praying to my puppets. Stunned, I stepped back again and slithered down the hall towards the kitchen. The one thing I had to do was get light before Susi called or came to look for me. I found and banged the copper gong, and returned like a shot out of a gun, back to stand in the bedroom door to stand between that ghost, or whatever it was, and Susi."

'Jan' I heard her say in a small voice of terror, 'Jan! Is that you, Jan?'

'Yes' I said, It's me. I can't find the torch so I rang for Tiap to find us some candles. I hope he hears.'

'Oh, Jan,' Susi pleaded, 'it doesn't matter. Lock the bedroom door and come to bed. Please come to bed. Please, Jan.'

But I stood like a rock in the doorway, with wide unblinking eyes staring into the hall, my prominent jaw protruding in a pose of belligerence above my solid chest which could not muffle the hard pounding of the heart beneath it. Seconds ticked by with the drag of hours.

Then there was a shuffling at the back door, a key in the lock, the reclosing of the door against the pressure of the wind, the unsatisfactory flicking of a light switch.

'Is that you, Tiap?' I called out. 'The power is out and we need a light.'

If he answered I did not hear against the sudden onslaught of tropical rain that deluged out of the thunderous clouds. But almost immediately a flicker of light appeared from the kitchen and came towards me where I stood at the door with perspiration dripping from my back to my pyjama trousers. Tiap had lighted candles in a tin, three-pronged candelabra which he held in his hand, reflected to double light against his white coat. I moved forward and took the candelabra from his hand.

'It is the breaking of the monsoon, Tuan,' Tiap said evenly, with the deliberate condescension a man uses to calm fear.

'I know,' I snapped. 'Get more lights. Nonja is concerned about the baby.'

And I went back into the bedroom, put the candelabra near Susi, who was sitting up rigid with her hand on the baby's cot. Then I removed one of the candles and, holding it in my hand, went without a word back across the hall into the living room. As I arrived there was a clap of thunder and a crash. But no ghost was waiting to receive me. One space on the puppet wall was empty and, as might have been expected, I bent to pick up the awkwardly heavy clown puppet that had fallen to the floor.

With the puppet in my free hand, I returned to Susi. Her reaction was astounding.

'What are you doing with that? Take it away! Take it away, Jan, do you hear? Don't put it near the baby.'

'It just fell down again, Susi, that's all. The wind, I suppose. It's the one you gave me.'

'I know what it is,' she whispered. 'I know what it is. I hate it. I won't have it in here with the baby. Take it away!'

I went to my wardrobe, pulled out a briefcase, opened it, put the puppet inside and turned the small key in the lock. Then I turned to console Susi. The wind was howling, the rain thundering down on the roof, but above these sounds of nature's violence I imagined I could hear her sobbing. But I was wrong. She had taken the baby into bed with her and was lying wide-eyed and tearless., staring straight ahead of her like a medium in a trance. I could still hear the sobbing or thought I could. Perhaps it was the whine of the gale in my imagination, but for all that it made me furious. I opened the bedroom door with a flourish and faced Tiap who stood waiting with another candle in each hand. How long, I wondered had he been standing there?"

'Tuan,' he muttered, 'I could not easily find more lights.'

'These will do,' I said and took both from his hands, 'if you can find your way out. The baby has gone to sleep again. We will not need you anymore.'

'Nothing for Nonja, Tuan?'

'No, thank you, Tiap. Good night.'

'I will remain in the house, Tuan.'

'That will not be necessary.'

'In the room of the puppets, perhaps?'

'Why?'

'Then in the kitchen, Tuan.'

He bowed and was gone like a shadow down the hall. I put down the candles, closed and quietly locked the bedroom door. Then I put all the candles together in a cluster of five on the table at my side of the bed. They cast a weird, waving travesty of light on the ceiling that reflected on the white pillow and Susi's blanched face.

'Put the candles out, Jan,' she whispered, 'put them out. The dark is better. Come back to bed.'

"There seemed nothing else to do but obey her. My restless and unsatisfied frustration was a weak and pointless reason for sitting up the rest of the night. I longed for a pipe, but Susi had begun to croon softly to the child in her arms. This I really could hear like a requiem above the rain, and I knew its somnolence should be enough for one night for one man. Questions could wait until the light of day.

But in the morning, Susi rose while I still slept to feed the baby and then excused herself sleepily from breastfeeding with me and had fallen into a deep sleep by the time I had showered. I resisted an unreasonable desire to shake her awake to talk to me; there are some things a man just cannot do.

Tiap was waiting for me at the dining table, twitching with an agitation made doubly noticeable in contrast to his usual demeanour.

'Tuan,' he said anxiously. 'One of the puppets has gone from the wall.'

'I know,' I said irritably. 'It fell down in the night. It is too heavy even for the last frame. I have put it away.'

'Put it away,' he repeated with blank urgency. 'Put it away. It is too heavy even for the last frame.' Then he noticed I was staring at him and recovered himself. 'You will put it back, Tuan?'

'Perhaps, but I am not sure.' I thought of Susi in the night. 'It does not match the rest of the collection. You must have noticed.'

He said, surprisingly, 'I have noticed, Tuan, that it was not made by an expert, which seemed impossible desecration.'

'What did you say?'

He bowed deliberately, hiding his face. 'The rest of your collection is perfect, Tuan.'

'That particular puppet was a gift from my wife when we were first married,' I informed him.

To my astonishment he sighed a long breath that sounded like the hiss of a bicycle tyre when the valve is removed, and I found myself watching him intently as I continued, 'She knew very little about puppets, apart from their dress, and thought the head was unusual.'

'Who sold it to her,, Tuan?'

'A man in the market right here in Jogja. We were here for a week's holiday,' I finished abruptly, whereupon he said softly:

'And Nonja took it back to Jakarta to surprise you with later, as a gift. That makes it difficult, Tuan.'

'Difficult? Why?'

'In other circumstances I would offer to take it from you to make a new head. As it is, Tuan, perhaps you will allow me to remodel it with less weight so the thunder will no longer threaten it in anger.'

'You? Do you make puppets?'

He bowed modestly. 'I was taught the art as a boy, Tuan.'

For a moment I was tempted to confide in him the figment of my imagination I had seen the previous night before the puppet fell, but I bit my tongue in time out of a sense of loyalty to Susi."

'Thank you, Tiap,' I said instead. 'As you say, it is difficult. I will have to consult my wife before I accept your offer.'

'It may be possible, Tuan, that the nonja prefers a new head. I will wait.'"

~

"It was most certainly possible that Susi would prefer a new head on the clown puppet, but I did not get a chance to ask her that question or any other that were waiting in my mind. All morning I fretted, past normal concentration, and eventually to get home a little earlier than usual for lunch. To my surprise, a smiling Susi was established in the living room on a chair actually facing the wall where the remaining puppets were displayed. She greeted me with an announcement that seemed to please her immensely.

'I have a surprise for you.' She beamed. 'Two, in fact. The first is that lunch is ready, even though you are early, because I have made it myself.'

'You have made it, but why, darling? Where is Tiap?'

'He asked for the morning off. His father sent for him from his desa. It seems his half-brother has returned unexpectedly from Jakarta for family reasons. He expects to be finished his share of the business by about four o'clock this afternoon and will return then. Things could not have turned out better.'

'You talk in riddles, Susi. In what way?'

'Because of the man who is coming this afternoon. He phoned just a few minutes ago, and I think it is better, seeing he is coming about the puppets, that Tiap is not here.'

'Why?'

'Because Tiap is such a nuisance about them, as you know very well, always guarding them and worshipping them.'

'Worshipping them? Did you say worshipping them?'

'Well, he does, Jan. I have seen him actually bowing to them as if they were alive.'

'Susi, why didn't you tell me this before?'

'Because it really doesn't matter very much if he does worship the puppets, does it? You do yourself in a different sort of way. I don't mind except for that ugly one that fell down. And that is the important thing, because the man who is coming this afternoon wants to buy the clown puppet.'

'Who is this man, Susi?'

'He is a merchant, and he got our name from that shop in Jakarta where you used to go to buy a puppet when you could afford it. You know – Mr Beerlug, who got the puppets from the Solo area. He is a friend of Mr Beerlug.'

'How do you know he wants to buy the clown puppet?'

'Well, you know the clown puppet is the strangest one we have ever seen. I don't know for sure, Jan, but I think the thing is just a little too strange. For some reason I have hated it ever since we put it up in this house, even if Tiap does give it the same treatment as the others.'

'Please keep to the point, Susi. This man who is coming – what makes you think he wants to buy our puppet?'

'He described it exactly over the telephone, Jan. It seems he had it made for him and was to have picked it up in the market in Jogja from the man who made it. But the man's son sold it by mistake to somebody else. That could be me, couldn't it?'

'It could be, but it sounds a pretty unlikely story,' I said dubiously.

'Well, the man says he collects what he calls macabre or gro-
tesque puppets, and ours certainly falls into the right category.
He says he has a note introducing him from Mr Beerlug.'

'Then why didn't he phone me at work?'

'He did, and as you had already left, they gave him the
telephone here.'

She paused and although by this time I realised that her
excitement was somehow tied up with extraordinary relief, I
felt compelled to hesitate on behalf of the puppet.

'But you know I love that puppet because you gave it to me,
Susi. Do you really want to sell it as much as all this? Did you
mean what you said last night?'

'I wish I had never bought it, Jan. It is a macabre puppet,
just like the man says. If he wants that kind of puppet, let him
have it – it doesn't fit here, Jan. There is something about it,
something sinister – it haunts the place.'

'You are sure it is not your imagination, Susi? Don't forget
that Tiap upset you when you first saw him. You are sure it is
not Tiap guarding the puppets that worries you?'

I hated myself for watching her so closely, but her answer
was as natural as the sun after rain.

'That was only because I thought he looked like the man
who followed me in Jakarta when I was first expecting the baby.
A man really did follow me, Jan, although you didn't believe me
at the time. I had to use all the ingenuity I had to avoid being
followed home, so it was natural, I suppose, to feel suspicious
afterwards of anybody the same size and shape. Of course, I
realise now that it could not have been Tiap since he was here
in Jogja. Shall we eat now, or do you want a drink first?'

She was already up and almost dancing towards the kitchen.
I felt stunned by her gaiety, which seemed to drop pieces
into a jigsaw puzzle I had not realised was there. Either she
was holding something back or I was an uncompromising fool.
Perhaps, I thought darkly, it was a case of both, for when Susi

came back she had the babu in tow to serve the lunch instead
of Tiap. Somehow, it proved to be impossible to question Susi
further and we had just taken our coffee in the living room
when the visitor arrived carrying a small suitcase.

I must admit at once that I was unprepared to like the man,
but to be fair, I found him affable, and he presented the letter
from my friend in Jakarta immediately and in a businesslike
manner without being asked for it. Everything he said substan-
tiated his remarks to Susi on the telephone, and I knew that
had he spoken to me, I would have agreed to see him if for
no other reason than his avowed interest in the collection of
puppets. His name was Groote and from his appearance he was
half Dutch and half Javanese. One might have described him as
a handsome man of the urbane variety, impeccably mannered
and well-dressed according to his European heritage, but with
a dash of suavity and reserve. He was, in other words, the kind
of man you met daily in business circles in the East but never
got to know very well. Anyway, I could not fault him, but I did
not like him, either. Neither did Susi, for she was suddenly the
formal hostess and housewife instead of a personality in her
own right, leaving all the conversation to me except to comment on the early monsoon and the sugar in the coffee she
offered to Groote as our guest.

Groote, accepting the coffee, flattered Susi with the ap-
praising eye some men reserve for that contrasting fragility of
blonde beauty that promote in them all the reserves of their
gallantry. During this formality of hospitality, I read the letter
of introduction from my friend Beerlug, and was surprised to
note that in case I wished to replace my puppet with the
guaranteed purchase of others from a reliable source, a considerable sum was already lodged to cover the transaction. If
I preferred cash, that also was at my disposal. Even further,
Beerlug intimated that if I felt the puppet was of greater value
to me than the proposed very generous offer, I should not

hesitate to say so as Groote was most anxious to secure the puppet for personal reasons. The intriguing point to me was that there seemed to be no doubt that the particular puppet, out of all the thousands in the island of Java, was in my possession.

I redirected Groote's attention to the matter of his visit and queried how he had managed to trace the ownership of the puppet, if indeed our puppet was the one he was after. His answer was straightforward and logical.

'The circumstances were in my favour,' he said. 'The man who sold the puppet remembered Madame.' He bowed in the direction of Susi, 'Which if I may say so with respect to yourself, Sir, is not surprising. The face of beauty is not easily forgotten. Tuan Beerlug recognised the description as resembling your wife. The puppet itself, I admit frankly, is unique and the only one of its kind carved in this manner by a colleague of mine, since deceased, for myself and sold by mistake to your wife. My reasons for regaining it are sentimental, as you will realise, and I am willing to give you your price.'

'The price you offer is more than adequate' I said, looking at Susi.

She took her cue immediately and stood up.

'The puppet will no doubt be happier where it belongs,' she said neatly and rang the little bell on the coffee table.

As Tiap had not yet returned, her intention was to have the babu clear away while I fetched the puppet. Groote, whose eye had already scanned the empty space on the wall, bowed and waited. I passed the babu hurrying out of the kitchen just as I reached our bedroom door.

'Is Tiap back yet?' I enquired. She was a happy little old-one and she grinned ingratiatingly, bowed and nodded. 'Now, Tuan,' she replied and hurried on to answer Susi's call.

For a moment I hesitated, wondering if I should wait to speak to Tiap before handing over the puppet. But I decided against the sudden thought. Susi had bought the puppet and Susi wanted to be rid of it. The offer was strange and gave me a guilty feeling of succumbing to greed. But surely, I reasoned, the circumstances were such that it was preferable to allow Susi to be rid of what she abhorred for the privilege of replacing it with a pre-paid new choice.

When I put the heavy wooden clown puppet into the outstretched hands of Groote, his hands trembled under the weight and just for a flick of a second I thought he would drop it.

'Careful!' I exclaimed. 'It is heavy for a puppet.'

He recovered and almost hugged the thing against his well-cut suit jacket while his eyes glittered into my own.

'Heavy,' he breathed, 'yes, it is heavy.'

Then he moved and the puppet disappeared into his bag with the speed of a snake disappearing into the grass. After that, I had the impression that Tuan Groote could hardly depart my house fast enough. Having politely taken him to the door, Susi and I returned to the living room where, from the vantage point of the window, we watched his controlled progress down our slippery, mud-spattered garden path. The sky was darkening for another downpour and a fitful preparatory wind was disturbing the shrubs and trees growing in profusion at the gate."

'He said he came in a betjak. I hope it waited for him. It is going to pour!' I remarked, putting my arm around Susi's waist. I felt her tremble as if a shiver ran up her spine.

'I hope so too,' she said. 'I couldn't bear it if he came back. There is something about him that exactly matches that puppet.'

Turning my head, I bent to kiss her lightly on the crest of her fair hair. As I did, I felt every muscle of her body suddenly stiffen.

'Jan,' she whispered. 'Oh my God, Jan. He has fallen over. Look!'

I looked and saw Groote spreadeagled just inside my garden at the already opened gate.

'Stay here, Susi,' I commanded and pounded out the front door.

Before I turned him over and saw the spreading stream of his blood, I knew he was dying. The hair rose on the back of my neck, for he had been cleanly stabbed and somewhere near in the sweltering fecundity of my shrubbery, his murderer was lurking. With an involuntary gasp I pulled back my hand from Groote's shoulder as I felt his body twitch and shudder. Then his eyelids lifted and seemed to focus on my face as I knelt on the path, and his lips shook and quivered as if he was stricken with fever.

'I could not get it away. I did not get it away,' he muttered, 'and it had the kris on it; my family – my family kris in it, the diamond kris – I did not get it. My brother took it back again – I did not get it – I did not get it.'

Then he shuddered just once as his eyes misted and his head lolled to one side against his hunched coat.

I scarcely know how I got back to the house, but I was on the verandah when I nearly fell over the babu staring out of the door with the baby in her arms.

'Give the baby to Nonja and get Tiap,' I ordered sharply.

'Not here,' the babu said anxiously.

'You said he was back!'

'Sorry, make mistake, Tuan. I see betjak man, same like Tiap, not Tiap. Tiap not come back from desa yet, Tuan.'

'He must be back! Go and see. Go now.'

Susi came out of the living room door and with her eyes searching my face, took the baby from the babu.

'I will have to phone the police, Susi,' I said. 'The man is dead.'

~

"Perhaps the most incredible thing about the whole affair was the attitude of the police, who were brief, courteous and gave the impression that the murder was the logical conclusion, rather than the beginning of an investigation. Naturally, Susi and I were filled with grave apprehension while we waited for their arrival, having decided to tell the simple truth without elaboration: that Groote had called with an introduction from a dealer in Jakarta to buy from us a puppet that we wished to sell because it did not match the rest of our collection. The police accepted this explanation of the man Groote's presence at our house as casually, it seemed to me, as they accepted his murder. Almost, it might have been suspected, with relief. They explained to us with unnecessary emphasis that they knew the man, who was not, as he pretended, a collector of puppets, yet I surmised from an odd remark that he was in some way related to a Javanese family who did collect them. He had, according to the inspector, operated under one of several assumed names with me, but paradoxically it turned out that he had acted in good faith with my friend Beerlug and had lodged the security to pay for the puppet in cash. Since I was not asked, I refrained therefore from repeating the dying remarks of the man which, since I was without witnesses, might or might not be considered valid in a court of law. Nor did I tell Susi, who was naturally distressed and upset by the final outcome of her one and only purchase of a puppet, that the clown I was asked to identify in the man called Groote's bag, was not in fact her puppet at all in any respect but dress. In the matter of identification, I agreed with Tiap, who had returned within the hour and stood on the front veranda beside me in his white coat, when the inspector opened the bag. Seeing Tiap nod his head wisely at the inspector's question, I did likewise. When the inspector further inquired whether I wished the puppet returned to me after the case was closed, I declined his offer, explaining that I thought the sight of it might distress my wife and remind her of the day's events. The inspector quite understood.

It was, of course, inevitable that Tiap would have to leave us. We were sorry to lose his service, for as I have remarked before, we will never again find a house boy of his calibre. The replacement we found was, in comparison, merely adequate but faithful, and remains with us still. Tiap explained to Susi that his father was very old and could no longer manage alone the affairs of his family. It was necessary that, according to ancestral custom and security, Tiap, as the eldest son, should return to the desa. Susi was kind but unlike the babu, showed no emotion whatsoever the day Tiap departed. For my part, I found myself extraordinarily moved when he presented as a parting gift, an exquisitely carved wooden puppet to fill the empty space on our living room wall. I did not embarrass him by offering a gift in an exchange already accomplished."

~

Absorbed, I sighed as Jan finished his story and fell into a long silence with my eyes on the thick, purple-green verdure around his garden gate.

"So that is the story of the beautiful puppet?" I said at last.

"The beautiful puppet?" Jan replied."Oh, no, that is the story of the clown puppet, the preliminary story, the reason why Susi admits no favourite and will have no clown puppets in the house. The story of the beautiful puppet is a sequel even more astonishing."

"Another shadow-play, Jan?"

"Exactly that, or perhaps reversed, into an even stranger play of shadows. After Tiap left, Susi grew very brave and even refused to return to Holland for the birth of our second son. Shortly after this splendid event I received an invitation to a performance of the Wayang in the gardens of a palace. Susi insisted that I go alone, for indeed, she rightly observed, I might never receive such an invitation again. I was, of course, one of many guests, but during the midnight laughter evoked by the clowns of Arjuna, an attendant tapped me on the shoulder and beckoned me to follow him. I was taken to a little room where puppets were arranged on the wall and invited to view them. It was the most splendid private collection I had ever seen, and I studied each in turn like a man in a trance for, as I have told you, the creatures are an obsession with me. One puppet, in spite of my best intentions, I touched, just lightly you understand, to caress the wood of the face. I withdrew my hand in horror at my audacity. The attendant did not appear to have noticed. I followed him out again into the garden just as the Sultan and his retinue were rising. In the half-light I suddenly stood transfixed, for surely the small man up in front beside the platform, bowing respectfully toward the departing royal entourage, was Tiap. Fascinated by such a unique possibility, I detoured to walk straight past him before returning to my seat. But as was to be expected, my imagination had run away with me for I was mistaken who allowed me to pass without the slightest sign of recognition.

About an hour later, a ceremonial box containing the puppet that I had touched and you admire, was placed in my hands as I left the palace. The members of the royal household, the attendant informed me, hoped I would accept the gift in celebration of the birth of my second son."

WANITA OF THE WATER-PIPE

The out-patients' queue in the hospital gardens was very long, and the family members accompanying the sick and injured were chattering gaily like brightly feathered parakeets as they arranged themselves for the day. It was seven in the morning; the sun was well up in the blue sky and there was only one hour to wait until the clinic opened and a smiling, white-gowned Sister received the first casualty who had been brought on a stretcher just after midnight. The food-vendor was busy serving a bowl of rice to the two betjak-drivers who had brought this patient in; their wives had sent the children to school and had come to replace them as they were anxious to ply their trade again to earn the day's food. One of them whistled softly no louder than a bird in order to both respect the hospital regulations and attract the attention of a small boy who had a bunch of finger-bananas to sell before he ran off to his primary class.

Ita sat down at the exact moment the sun left the grass at the root of an enormous hibiscus shrub just inside the hospital gate. She had waited over an hour for the queue to reach this location, which would place her inside the shade but not bring her to the door of the waiting-room until the late afternoon. She was a very pretty girl. Already she had bathed in the nearest canal and washed the faded sarong in which she had slept, drying it in the sun on the grassy slope before she folded it neatly to put in her bundle that she now placed open beside her. She was very careful of her bundle, which represented all her worldly possessions: the second sarong, a small, square bark cloth, a coconut-shell rice bowl, a small Arjuna puppet-doll, and, because she was a modern girl, a plastic cup, a comb, a mirror and a lipstick in a flat rattan purse. The purse also contained a child's spelling book and a crayon, but her greatest treasure she kept in an old skin pouch that hung around her neck to rest hidden above her breasts. It was here she kept the hospital card, the tiny photograph of herself and Sopari taken by the man under a black hood on the day they met. The pouch also held the ten rupiah Sopari had given her for the baby, four months ago before he was arrested in the riots. Sopari was an educated boy who had learned to read and write before he left his village to find work in Jakarta. He had recognised immediately that Ita was a girl from a good family that was still too old-fashioned and honest to think that anything but evil could come from offering education to a girl so eligible to make a good marriage. Nowadays, Sopari told Ita, parents no longer had the right to arrange a wedding without consulting the wishes of the daughter. He himself, Sopari, a modern Indonesian, would teach Ita to read and write, and as soon as he had a regular job they would be married and set up a proper household. Even if he nearly starved to do it, he would give her ten rupiahs every week so that she would have enough to have their baby in a hospital with modern medical care. There was no use fighting for the new Indonesia if their child were to die through the carelessness of an untrained midwife in some kampong.

Ita smiled as she opened her bundle with her right hand, careful not to jar her left arm to pain beneath the bandage, which she had held so adroitly above the water of the canal. Sopari, in his wisdom, told her how infectious germs lurked in the still, filthy water and had shown her the new water-pipes that were waiting in the streets beside the gutters to take the beautiful new water from the hills into every house when they were laid. It was lucky he had told her; how else would she have known how to re-infect her wounded arm just two weeks before her baby was due and get herself a card for hospital treatment. You could not get an admission card for just a baby, or for an infection, for that matter. But if you had been brought in after a riot with a knife wound to the bone, you were treated for two months and your name went on a list so that if your wound went infectious again you could come back. She had been coming back every day for fourteen days and every day she had dipped her arm into the water of the canal, but not this morning. Last night, as she lay in her shelter, breathing in the smell of the rain with her head on her bundle and the mangoes beside her, her body had leapt with a new agony, only to quieten again. It had happened again in the morning, and she knew her time had come.

The bundle had been difficult to tie, for it was bulky with the twelve mangoes she had stolen instead of the usual ten. For the same reason it was easy to untie, and she was glad to place them one by one on her little cloth on the grass in front of her. If she sold them quickly, she would have enough to buy a bowl of rice from the vendor with a spoonful of dried flaked fish. Yesterday she had done without the fish and traded two mangoes she could not sell for four bananas. She hoped that today she could sell the mangoes fast and eat all the food at once instead of spreading it out all day, making the pressure of her stomach hasten her labour into the daylight hours when they would have to take her in. She was only sixteen years old, and she dared not think of the hours after the hospital gates were closed. She raised her voice in a high, sweet treble. "Mangga begitu bagus-murah sekali – such fine mangoes, very cheap."

~

My luncheon was at Nono Wirojo's house, in honour of her cousin from the Celebes. She lived on a narrow street in a beautiful garden, shaded with many trees so that it was difficult to see the house from the street. Everybody familiar with the locality parked their car on the next crossroad and walked the distance to Nono's gate, so Titi told me. In the end, her explanation was so complicated I begged her to come with me herself, which she did, so it was with Titi that I sauntered between the overgrown green shrubs and the black water-pipes that lined Nono's footpath. I was amazed, for often we had to walk single file, and several times bumped the solid cast-iron of the pipes, which seemed almost as tall as Titi.

"Fancy leaving the water-pipes here," I said, "there's no room left on the road, let alone the path."

"For more months than a year is big problem," Titi explained, "and no plenty good water for Nono, only much promises. But it is better than no thing to see. Some day will come."

I did not disillusion her, for like Nono she suffered water-rationing every day of her life, and sometimes the supply was cut off altogether. Jakarta had a population of over three million people and all the public services were designed for half a million. I feared it would take a long time for pure water to flow freely into every home from the water-pipes. But I hoped for Nono's sake that the pipes in her street would be laid among the first laid.

It was true you could scarcely see Nono's house for the trees. The garden was an orchard of tropical fruit grown together in profusion that blocked out the sun. At the gate was a mango tree pressed hard against paw-paw and pamplemousses with shaggy bananas, sugar-palm and pineapple fronds struggling for space between. The rich, spicy aroma of mango mingled with the sweet scent of jasmine. Titi and I walked towards the verandah where Nono greeted us, surrounded by her guests.

"How shady it is in your garden," I said to Nono, "and so quiet. It is like being out in the country."

"Nono grows the best mangoes in Jakarta," one of the guests said.

Nono laughed. "Which you will have for your lunch, what is left of them. For my "usband is dis-a-strus. Somebody is stealing the mangoes."

"Have you set a watch?" Titi asked. She adored a mystery.

"No watch yet, my 'usband too tired, - too many peoples sick alla time. He say, maybe watch tonight for thief or tell police. Not let me watch. Much danger now. My 'usband think somebody sleep in water-pipe. Very bad man, maybe, just out of lock-up. Very clever for hiding."

"For stealing the beautiful mangoes, you mean," Titi teased her. "Every year somebody steals the mangoes."

"But not just little few every night, ripe ones. And the letter come to our box, ver-ry strange, have our street, our number, but not our name."

All the Indonesian ladies cried, "A letter!" and then their tongues, full of excitement flowed gaily back to their natural Bahasa spoken with such rapidity I could not catch a word. Soon we went in to lunch and the sight of the whole fish baked in bamboo, the enormous bowls of fruit salad, the tempting smell of fresh-fried krupuk and bananas in spice batter eliminated every thought of a few stolen mangoes. It was only on the drive home that I remembered to ask Titi what was in the letter.

~

By noon the hospital queue had moved forward faster than Ita, in her anxiety, had anticipated. She had sold all the mangoes but three, traded two for bananas, eaten all the purchased food and waited for her stomach to exert pressure on her womb. But only once in five hours waiting had pains assailed her. At half-past twelve she offered her place in the queue to the old man with the retching cough who was suffering the sun in the place she had just vacated. In a few minutes she would do the same for the lady who had brought two children for injections to heal their aching sores caused by yaws. By one o'clock she had moved back five places, only to be replaced by the attendant who belligerently checked the cards for the afternoon clinic, which began at two. For a dreadful hour this well-fed, immaculately uniformed hospital servant exerted his important authority over his less fortunate fellows. Ita felt like asking if he had heard the Pancasila, the wonderful new code of rights on which the new Indonesia was based. Sopari had made her memorise it: Love of God; Humanity; National Consciousness; Democracy; Social Justice for All. That was what Sopari was demonstrating for when the march was turned into a riot that took Sopari's freedom. Ita had no doubt that it was men like this attendant who were really responsible for the violence. She knew the look in the eyes of a man who would trail a decent girl like herself along the streets of Jakarta. Several times he had mocked her, asking where her husband was while she sat in the hospital grounds and once, a week ago, he had offered to move her up in the queue. Back in her original place, between the old man and the talkative woman with the children, she put the last mango back in her bundle and tied it up, keeping out only her thin spelling book and the crayon. Her heart was not as usual in her learning, not since the day she had gone without food and written her first letter to Sopari with the carefully copied address in it, and bought a stamp and sent it to the jail. There had been no reply. She did not know where Sopari was and he did not know where she was. Her back ached worse than her arm and she felt dizzy. The food-vendor had gone outside the gate, back to his stall to prepare more rice over his coal fire and cook anew with fresh herbs his aromatic stew. The smell filtering into the hospital gardens hit Ita's nostrils and made her feel sick. It was too pungent, she tried to tell herself, he was masking the lack of meat with too much pepper-seed. Really, she knew this was the only way the food-vendor could earn enough to feed his family. He had been generous with his spoonful of dried fish when he knew she could not afford the stew. It was fear that was making her sick. In two hours she would be in the waiting room. The baby was not going to come in time. She had a sudden desperate urge to walk, even to run, and stood up violently, her whole body shaking with the effort. The woman with the two children looked at her strangely and stood up also, her youngest child whimpering, half asleep in her arms.

"Don't jump like that," the woman said to Ita. "If it's your first and you sit quiet, you'll be able to get home in time. This isn't a maternity hospital. They won't let you stay here. But they might give you something to make it easier if you wait your turn."

Ita stared at the thin, strained face of the woman and then lowered her eyes to the head of the child as she forced herself to answer.

"It hasn't started," she lied. "I don't feel anything. I just want to walk, that's all. I just want to walk."

The attendant had ushered the first eight afternoon patients into the waiting room and, under the surveillance of the reception Sister, was benevolently keeping back the relatives from blocking the door. Ita began to walk.

"I'll keep your place," the woman called out after her, and moved up and settled herself again, shunting the weight of the child in her arms. The second child dropped beside her listlessly, refusing the banana she offered.

Ita kept moving as long as she could, back and forth, trying to look inconspicuous by keep her head high and swinging her bundle. Most of the people in the queue were feigning sleep. Once, a man with a bandaged head inquired if her arm ached and she told him it was driving her crazy. An hour later, when the dizziness overcome her, she dropped under a tree by the gate and wept. After that she felt temporarily relieved and closed her eyes and thought about the happiness she had shared with Sopari. She was roused by the hand of the woman who was keeping her place.

"Hurry, come quick," the woman said, "you're the last of the next lot to go in. Then there's only us and the last three." She was very excited.

"They say only one injection will fix my children. Only one. Do you think it is magic inside the syringe? A woman told me when you have the needle either you died or are well right away. Two children died in our kampong after a needle."

"They would have died anyway," Ita said, "and I know for sure because I was told by an educated man that hundreds have the needle and get well. It is not magic, it is true medicine, not like the herb man in the village gives you. You take my place. I don't mind. I don't hurt now. Go on. Hurry up."

The woman ran like the wind back to her wailing children. Ita picked up her bundle and slowly, painfully, with stiff controlled movement approached the diminishing queue. The woman and her children disappeared through the door. The attendant considered himself tired and frustrated at the end of a trying day's work, unappreciated by the hospital clientele.

"You can just take the end of the queue," he said haughtily to Ita, "since you preferred to leave your place and sleep under a tree."

She scarcely heard him as she dropped to the grass and sat rocking gently like an over-ripe mango, newly fallen from the tree. Her even white teeth bit into the firm flesh of her lip as she moaned a little, refusing to cry out.

~

I was reminded of the letter when we passed Nono's mango tree on the way out to her narrow street blocked with water-pipes, but I said nothing about it as nearly all the other ladies accompanied us as far as their cars parked a block away on the main road turnoff beside the canal. I only had a minute or two to ask in the car because Titi had a message to deliver to her husband from Nono's husband, which was not to be telephoned.

"You are sure you don't mind stopping with the note?" Titi said as we drove off "It won't take long and must have to do with medical supplies. I know very well that if I not take it Nono goes walking in hot sun with it, not safe for boy to take this."

"Of course I don't mind," I answered. "Anyway, it is only a block or two, Nono said. It is a pity her husband doesn't go there instead of yours." And to change the subject as well as satisfy my curiosity I asked about the letter.

Titi laughed. "Nono showed it to prove how strange, – like a child write it – all like print in schoolbook, very short."

"What did it say?"

"Just four lines: 'very happy your letter, be back five weeks, meet in front of water-pipe, bring baby.' You see? Just child playing games. Nono is silly to think of bad people, it is because of the mangoes. It is always same; somebody steal her mangoes. Here we are!"

Indeed we were, right in front of the hospital.

"Oh, good," Titi said, "not so busy, all patients at clinic finished early. Come in with me and see my husband, he will be pleased. It will be cool in waiting room. Do come. I will bring him from surgery."

"But, Titi, he may be busy."

"No, only half-past four and nearly finished, nobody waiting outside. It has been a good day. I know. Come."

She was quite correct in her deductions. There was only one lady left in the waiting room. The reception Sister was delighted to see Titi and took her to find the doctor. I made myself comfortable in one of eight rattan chairs that ran around the wall, winding up at the reception desk. It was only then I took a look at the one remaining patient and was startled into looking again. She was literally huddled in the chair nearest the desk. Her left arm was heavily bandaged and lay across her swollen body, which was shaking uncontrollably. Her head was sunk deep into hiding under her raised arm. Only her chin was visible and her lower lip was bleeding. My reaction was quite automatic. I rose and slipped into the chair beside her and, as I did, she dropped her arm and lifted her face. She was very young, not much more than a girl, and her pale, strained face was very beautiful, small and delicately moulded like a Balinese carving; but her great dark eyes were sad eyes, dumb and dull with pain. I realised at once that she was in labour, and at almost the same moment sprang up and pressed the bell on the desk. When I turned again to the girl she was sitting up straight in her chair, looking straight ahead, all of her body controlled and quiet, her right arm supporting her bandaged left, and on her mouth the tiniest trace of a smile. She was sitting in exactly the same position when the Sister rushed in.

I did not speak good Bahasa, so it was with difficulty that I tried to explain why I had run the bell, and with equal difficulty that the Sister tried to explain to me that this was not a maternity hospital, which I already knew. Also, for the Sister, it was the end of a long day and finally to escape from me she picked up the girl's card from the file on her desk and turned to address her.

"Ita Sopari?" she queried.

The girl nodded her head. Then, to my astonishment, the Sister read out the address from which I had just come. I might not have been sure, but the girl gave no sign that she had heard. The Sister slowly and yet sharply repeated the words. Again, the girl nodded. Perhaps because I looked startled, or perhaps merely because I was a friend of the doctor's wife, the sister smiled at me and said, "Terima kasi, Nonja. Thank you,

Madame," as she walked from behind the desk, helped the patient to her feet, and took her by the arm into the surgery. Absolutely dumbfounded, I stood in the waiting room on one foot and then the other until Titi returned with the doctor behind her. By the time I had finished my story, Titi's eyes were glowing with suppressed excitement and the doctor had walked behind the desk to pick up the card.

"Ita Sopari," he said. "Ita Sopari. I wonder if she is the girl brought in the night of the riots with a gash in the arm. She was pregnant. If that's the one I remember, she hesitated when she gave her name. She was scared, of course. Anyway, we will find out." He turned toward the surgery door.

"Don't forget to ask about the mangoes," Titi called after him in a loud whisper. Then she turned to me. "What a nuisance," she said. "He was all finished and coming home with us. Just the same, is exciting. Nono will have on me a good joke, you will see."

"Don't worry, Titi," I told her definitely. "We're going to wait. I want to know what happens to that girl."

"Me too." Titi nodded.

We did not have long to wait. The doctor came out smiling in a very few minutes with the Sister a little chagrined behind him.

"You were right about the girl," he informed us, "she should have her baby in a couple of hours. We can't give her a bed here, but my driver will take her over to Maternity. They can fit her in."

"Did she steal the mangoes?" Titi demanded.

"She did. She has been living on the sale of the mangoes for the last two weeks and sleeping in the water-pipe in front of Nono's house."

"But that's incredible," I cried. "That pretty little girl, in her condition, in the water-pipe!"

"And what will Nono say?" Titi gasped.

"That she can spare the mangoes when she hears the story. Nono has a big heart."

"Oh, yes," Titi said. "Nono has a big heart."

I did not realise just how big until Titi told me a week or so later that Ita sent a message of thanks for the quick collection of baby clothes I sent along to the hospital and hoped to see me one day while she was working in Nono's kitchen, where she would wait until Sopari came to that address to collect her.

REMORSE IS ABSENT

"All is bad," Amy Ling said, "bad for me, bad for Penny, cry all day. What to do?"

Amy sat stiffly upright on a chair in my living room. Her usually affable face, puffed with distress, made her black eyes seem as small and glittery as two beads. Her plump cheeks crinkled wistfully into as many creases as a violently deflated brown paper bag. I offered Amy another cup of tea and all the compassion possible until I was honoured with further confidences.

"Mother-in-law beat Penny, beat with stick every day. The good father say, 'Go back.' Penny say, 'die first'. Father of Penny say, 'must go'. I say, 'Not go'."

Amy, whose husband and Penny's father, I had noticed addressed her as Ah Me, was one of the Chinese ladies in the English conversation class who avoided the third person pronoun peril by scrupulous circumvention. On this particular morning Amy's voice had acquired a high, cheeping quality of forlorn monotony rather like the cry of a mother bird whose nest had been ravaged.

"But what about Penny's husband?" I asked. "Can't he stop his mother beating Penny?"

"No try, not at all." Amy sighed. "Mother wise for son – very clever – talk behind Penny – lies, big lies. No use Penny talk at all."

"Doesn't he love her?"

"Love when Penny get son. Wait for son. What now when baby come?"

"Is Penny expecting, Amy?"

"Very soon, maybe September – first child."

"Has she been married a long time?"

"Only little time – one year. Wedding beautiful, all white like Christian wedding, very rich, everything."

"Did she have a Church wedding?" Amy was a Christian Chinese, which was why both she and her daughter had Western names.

"No, bridegroom's family not Christian. But Penny good Christian girl, very good school. I told you. Learn good English, very special English speaking. Dutch too. Not speak Dutch now – put way now."

"Then why on earth didn't she marry a Christian?"

The small, black half-hidden eyes regarded me plaintively, as if my ignorance was almost too much to ask anyone carrying such grief to bear. Had I learned nothing during six months in Indonesia?

"The husband of me not Christian. The husband of mother of me not Christian. Father of me made wedding for me. Father of Penny made wedding for Penny."

"Did the Priest come, Amy?"

"Send nice invitation – gold edge – not come." Amy looked about to sob again.

I couldn't think what to say or what to do, and without doubt, Amy, expecting that I would do something, had come to me in the hope that being foreign and Christian I would give practical advice, even suggest a way out of her impasse. So, in order to give myself time to cultivate my innermost oracle, I made a tentative suggestion.

"Would your husband let you bring Penny to see me?"

"But of course. Why not, is modern man."

Confounded, I smothered my instinctive indignation in a mouthful of tea. Then I passed Amy a plate of small cakes and asked her when she would bring her daughter to visit me.

"After tomorrow, maybe, when Penny comes read English with class. You will see if you like."

I was a little amazed to learn in this manner that if Penny was coming to the English class, all the ladies already knew of her predicament. My further perception informed me that Penny would be at the English class to see if she would care to talk privately to me, not in order that I should agree to see her. My answer to the problem of Penny had better be astute, for it threatened to make me an unwilling hyphen between East and West. Marriage being universally binding, I could think of no Western wisdom erudite enough to embrace such deviation, and yet here was Amy, and probably other members of the English class, requiring of me the interpretation needed to indoctrinate the mothers of an ancient tradition into the mysteries of living in the modern world of human rights and equality of the sexes as demanded by their daughters. Knowing that Penny's problem was as unanswerable in the West as it was in the East, I could feel nothing but trepidation at the very thought of facing Penny at the English class where every member was the mother of a new generation daughter.

Not so Amy, who quite suddenly passed the burden of Penny into my lap as if completing a real estate contract on the principle that stunned silence is consent. Her whole face burst into a smile of complete confidence.

"Thank you," she said, "all is good, my feelings all better now. A friend is a mother. You are to all a mother."

Her faith was touching. It was consoling to know that whatever the future might hold, Amy Ling would enjoy a good night's sleep.

~

The class was at the home of Liti, in her charming, shaded house set modestly back from a street named after an island in the Celebes. Liti, being a Minangkabau, reflected the artistic heritage of her ancestry in her home in the same dainty way it abided in her person. In Liti's living room, re-arranged for the circle of deep rattan chairs, the table and the buffet pushed back against the walls, presented exquisite arrangements of flowers on bark and driftwood above delicate, hand-made Minangkabau lace. All over the East, women have so cultivated the art of flower arrangement that simplicity and beauty of presentation is as natural as them to sleep.

Framed in the window-seat, underneath a magnificent specimen of philodendron that was trained around the screened, glassless window instead of the foolishness of Western-style curtains, sat my friend Amy Ling, her cousin Rosy Wang, and between them a girl who could be none other than Penny. The two Chinese mothers wore charming examples of the Indonesian Chinese dress, based on the sarong of the islands in a slightly more pastel coloured batik skirt and topped with a cheerful cummerbund which wound from bosom to the waist under a sheer, elaborately embroidered blouse that identified the subtle differences between the dress of Javanese women and the Indonesian Chinese.

The pretty little girl who sat between my two friends, however, was a creature from another, less recognisable world. Contrasting the two smooth, sculptured heads of her elders, her hair bobbed gaily in a mass of short, hairdressers' curls. Her little mouth was fully as round and as red as a cherry plum, and her shining black eyes were magnified by the added darkness of mascara. She wore a loose sleeveless dress of scarlet silk, which flowed around her in voluminous folds before it was tucked in neatly a little below her knees. Her tiny feet in white sandals hung slightly above the floor. Had her feet been hidden under the folds of her dress, had she been sitting cross-legged on the window-seat, she would have introduced to the company a perfect resemblance of a round painted Buddha. She stood up with her mother as I walked toward her, and as she did I saw that she was so tiny the growing child within her took precedence over her whole body. She seemed to sway precariously on her feet. In this condition, apparently, she had seized her opportunity to walk home from a village some fifteen kilometres from Jakarta!

"I am very pleased to meet you," Penny said. "Mother had told me all about you."

"I am so glad you have come to the class," I replied, "even if, as is plain to see, you do not need to improve your English conversation."

"I came to meet you," she said, and when she smiled dimples indented the smooth outline of her porcelain cheeks.

Conscious of the sudden silence in the room, there flooded over me the realisation that the ladies of the conversation class, who had been greeting one another in buzzing groups, had lighted upon their seats in the circle like seagulls waiting for the turn of the tide. All the bright black eyes of the Indonesian-born were focused on myself and Penny. Though I knew my next words would be savoured as dew on parched grass, no supreme wisdom suitable for this occasion suggested itself to me. Like all women facing a similar predicament, I fell back upon the irrefutable ally of the unprepared which we call time. Smiling at Penny, I wave my hand airily around the circle of occupied chairs.

"It seems everybody is ready to start," I said. "I'll see you later, Penny."

"OK." Penny replied, and I detected a tiny spark like a flash of summer lightning in her eyes. She sat down for all the world like a red feather cushion resting with precarious abandon on the edge of a chair.

The English class preferred a valiant struggle through a good short story to a school-type lesson from a standard textbook. Each member in turn would read aloud a single page while the others underlined in their own copy, vocabulary and grammatical structure unknown to them. Reading, interspersed with pronunciation correction was an ordeal to be endured perhaps once in three weeks, for it was quite impossible to cover more than four pages at one sitting. At the end of a page, unknown words and phrases bounced like a ball around the group to be caught for identification in a dictionary marked English-Bahasa English-Dutch-French-English.

On this morning the first two pages were conversational and easy. At the end of the reading of the third page, Amy flew in like a comet with the word 'absent' almost before the reader had finished the sigh of relief that always accompanied the reading of the final phrase.

Startled, my eyes flew to Amy's impassive face. Every other eye in the room fastened itself on Penny.

"Absent is an easy word," I said as calmly as I could. "It simply means gone away for a while. There is only one more page to this story. Shall we read it so we can discuss the story as a whole?"

In the ensuing silence I waited for the reply of the ladies who eyed me with twinkling, knowing eyes.

"Or shall we have an essay." I sparked back at them. "Who has brought an essay today?"

There was a groan. Reading one's essay was even less popular than reading a page of the story, not because the essays were unprepared, but to read one's own masterpieces aloud was to be deprived of the joy of listening to someone else's. The current batch of essays was based on the subject of childhood memories, so listening to them was a fascination for all and the discussion of the contents hilarious fun.

"Amy has one," a voice called out.

"No, No!," Amy's voice was horrified. "Not this day, not this day."

Everybody giggled to cover their embarrassment at seeing the point so clearly.

"There is another word here I don't know," Liti put in, trying to exert her hostess privilege of diplomacy.

"On this page – no can't find – can't find. Finish story next week – very good idea. Reading last page gives much time left to talk about story."

She was quite right, of course. Knowing the quality of intellect possessed by the members of the class, it was inevitable that next week's lesson would involve a full discussion of the characters and plot of the story almost concluded. Having heard most of it read through, the ladies would re-read it at home, use their own dictionaries and be ready to apply practical, critical judgement to the actions of the characters. I knew well enough that with the exception of the one word lost by Liti, which she would track down with the tenacity of a small terrier and present at the most unlikely moment, the class had mentally postponed the story to the next session. This morning, in the minds of my friends, if not in my own, was reserved for another problem. I glanced at Amy, whose face was puckered into an apprehensive frown, and Penny, whose bright eyes shone as enigmatic and watchful as the gaze of an owl. Then I met the glance of Liti, whose expression told me plainly that I might as well let nature take it's course. It was obviously quite impossible to avoid the inevitable.

"Just as you like," I said ruefully. "We won't wait for your lost word, Liti. We all know you will find it and present it with the coffee when we are finished the class. Now, who has an essay?"

Liti giggled and all the ladies shuffled their feet.

"Rosy Wang has one," Milka said with the quiet distinction of a Javanese princess, allowing me to understand quite definitely that all their members had abdicated in favour of the Chinese.

Rosy was shy, which meant that her spoken English was less adequate than her comprehension. She might stutter as she pronounced the written word, but the content of her essays, grammar notwithstanding, like the alertness of her mind, never ceased to stagger me. Once again, I was not disappointed.

"So sorry," Rosy said, and opened her handbag for all to see its emptiness. She threw one dainty hand above her head in a gesture of despair.

"My house this morning – mad. My 'usband car juice all gone." Then like a staccato cicada she trilled off rapidly into Bahasa.

Around me the ladies gasped, their eyes round as oranges at the scandal. As Rosy stopped, giggled a little, apologised and attempted to finish her story in the foreign tongue.

"Poor man, came back in house, shouting – 'car no —'." She stopped and looked around for aid.

"Gas," Liti prompted.

"Gaz," Rosy repeated, "and time gone too far past sick peoples."

"Oh dear," I said. "Was your husband late for the hospital? Was he operating?"

"Very terrible," Rosy said, "telefon for 'ospital, telefon for car for my 'usband. Then gaz came back."

"How?" Liti demanded.

"Only go for lend, cook say."

"What, your cook stole the gas right out of the car?"

"Oh no, no, no. Satuorang – one – man – visit cook – brother of father in kampong. Cook put back juice quick in car and tell my 'usband gaz not gone – only little while – absent." Rosy sat back, her eyes twinkling a million sparks into my own.

"I have found him," Liti announced. "Here he is – the word: re-morse."

"Here it is, Liti," I corrected. "A noun is neutral, neither masculine nor feminine. Only persons are 'he' or 'she' in English."

Milka said with persuasive finality aimed at me: "'He' is a man, 'she' is a woman and all other things are 'it'."

"Which is quite right," Penny cried out. "He is a man and she is a woman. We Chinese are very silly to mix them up like we do as if both are the same, which is not true. The father is not the same as the mother, the sister is not the same as the brother, and every one of us knows the wife is not the same as the husband. It is lies to pretend. The man is boss and the woman is not."

Astounded, we covered embarrassment with laughter, not at Penny's words but at Penny herself, bouncing in indignation upon the window-seat. Yet it crossed my mind that I, as the only Western woman present, was easily the most perturbed.

Rosy replied at once on behalf of the Chinese mothers: "I see – for English language," she said. "For Chinese – all is same. Chinese son is man, but mother of son is woman. Earth and water grow rice. Who is boss, not big importance."

"It is important. It must be important to be fair," Penny said and looked straight at me. "Do you think it is, please?"

Stillness resting on the hot humid air was mirrored in the eyes of the mothers. This was the moment upon which my usefulness to Penny depended. What could I say to this girl approaching motherhood who was balanced in the no-man's land between two worlds?

"A man and a woman are not the same, Penny, but complementary to one another. There should be no boss of either sex in a home but truly balanced equality and love. This perfection exists in some homes, both in the East and in the West, but for most people it is only an accepted hope, Penny, not a daily reality."

"You have more equality than we have," Penny accused.

"Only because we have been working towards it longer."

"So," Rosy's voice sang out in sudden interruption, "not important."

From Penny the eyes swung to Rosy, whose cheeks flushed pink in two little spots on her high cheekbones.

"Liti's word," she said. "Liti's word – not find – not here in—." Helplessly, she held out her dictionary spread wide open in her hands.

We all cried out together in relief and laughter.

"Dictionary."

Solemnly, Rosy nodded her head. "Not here," she repeated, "no can find word – in deek-shon-ary. – Remorse is ab-sent."

~

The following afternoon, Penny was dressed in another costume: slim black Chinese trousers topped with a sleeveless garment cut on exactly the same lines as the red silk, only shorter and peacock blue. This time, with only myself present, Penny's sandals decorated my carpet as she sat cross-legged on the lowest chair in my parlour. The Buddha was blue.

"I won't go back," Penny said. "I will kill myself first."

"That's a bit drastic," I replied. "What a lovely shade of blue that is."

She ran her miniature ringless hand over the material. "I made this," she said.

"She took away my clothes. I came back in a sarong."

"A sarong?" I echoed.

"Belonging to one of the maids. She came too – the maid, I mean. She hates her as much as I do."

"But what about your husband, Penny?"

"I told him I would leave. I told them both. That's why she hid all my clothes. I don't care; I've made a new lot."

"You don't love your husband, Penny?"

A strange, puzzled expression fluttered across her eyes and then was gone. "No, not like you mean."

"What made you marry him?"

"He's the eldest son. I was number one wife, over all his brothers' wives."

"Are his brothers married, then? I thought— "

"That the eldest son married first. My husband's first wife died. I don't wonder. She came from Surabaya. That's too far to walk back."

"Did she have any children?"

"Only girls."

"You're a girl, Penny."

"And I hope I have a girl."

I smiled. "So do I, if she's as pretty as you are."

"It doesn't pay," Penny said, blinking her long lashes.

"Oh, I don't know," I said.

"It doesn't pay," Penny repeated flatly.

"You get spoiled. Then you think you have to have a number one son. You have to be number one wife. You have to be rich. The rich men want you, like rich fat girls want good-looking boys."

"Surely you had some choice in this day and age, Penny. You might have married a university boy or the son of one of the Christian merchants."

"I didn't know any."

"What about school?"

"Convent."

"But when you left?"

"We moved here from Semarang."

"So you came out, so to speak, in Jakarta."

"I didn't come out at all. I just got married."

"But you could have waited, surely, for a little while at least."

"What for? I didn't know any Chinese girls who waited or any Chinese boys to wait for me."

"Look, Penny, with your education you could have taken a job or trained yourself for some profession."

"A job or a profession is not the way to be number one wife to a rich husband. He wouldn't want a girl who had a job or a profession."

"I see. Well, you may have to think about a job now, Penny, if you don't go back."

"I'm not a respectable woman now. It doesn't matter."

"Don't be so silly, of course you're a respectable woman."

"Not if I don't go back. I won't go back. I'd rather kill myself than go back."

"Don't talk like that, it's silly."

"Why is it silly? If I go back, I would die, like the other one did – only slow. What's the difference?"

"The difference is that you are a bright, intelligent and beautiful woman. After you have your baby, you will have to make a new life for yourself – a modern life in a modern world. With your English you might get a job in an embassy, or you can train as a nurse."

"A nurse!" She looked scandalised, horrified.

"Or you can study and get into university, and after a while you can marry again."

"Never," Penny said.

"But why not? With the new laws, you could."

"Never," Penny said. "I don't like marriage. I hate it."

"How old are you, Penny?"

"Eighteen, the day I ran away."

"You're young enough to change your mind. In my country most girls don't think of getting married until they are at least twenty-one."

"What do they do?"

"Get a good education for a profession, or the experience working for a living provides. Only a very few nowadays just put in time entertaining themselves until they marry."

"I should think not," Penny said. "By the time they are twenty-one there wouldn't be a rich man left."

"The modern idea is to marry for love, not money or social position – though you may be lucky and have these things as well."

"Chinese make sure of luck."

On this conundrum we sat in silence, both thinking our own thoughts. Penny spoke again before I did.

"You think I do not need to go back or kill myself, then, to be a respected person?"

"That's my Western point of view."

"Even if the baby is a boy?"

"I don't think that makes any difference."

"I have to give the baby back if it's a boy – to her to bring up."

"Why? Is that the law?"

"The law?" Penny queried. "I don't know. But I might as well anyway."

"You could fight to keep your baby, legally I mean, if your parents can afford to."

"I beg your pardon!" Penny said.

"If your husband goes to the police court to try to get the baby back. You could say your mother-in-law beat you."

"How would that help?" Penny enquired. "The mother-in-law is always cruel. My husband is rich. He can give many presents."

"I see what you mean," was all I could answer, for this was dangerous ground.

"It wouldn't be worth it anyway," Penny said, with kindly condescension towards my thoughtlessness. "When he grew up my son would hate me – disgraced mother – himself disinherited."

"Penny, by the time he grew up he would be a well-educated citizen of the new Indonesia."

"Without Chinese."

"What did you say?"

"The new Indonesia won't have Chinese. Didn't you know?"

"I have no reason to agree with that possibility," I said carefully, "but under exceptional circumstances you could take your son to Singapore. There are many educated Chinese women in Singapore who are quite independent. You speak perfect English, you could be as they are, and work as they do."

"The baby's father will say to my father, 'Give me my son, heir to my wealth.'"

"But your father has no son."

"No, poor man, only me."

"Then your son can be heir to your father's wealth."

"Much, much less than my husband's riches."

"Then a baby boy might be safer with your father."

She was as quick as lightning to see this point.

"You think the richest will be ordered out first?"

"It is possible, if anyone is ordered out, which is very doubtful, you know, Penny,"

"Stripped of wealth, then, which is the same thing," she said with finality, having suddenly made up her mind with the mixture of shrewdness and glee of a martyr. "I have heard the merchants talk; I know."

Her eyes sparkled as her mind raced far ahead of mine with jabs of fiery comprehension. "If I go back to my husband, I would not be so safe either. If I send my baby back, he will be in great danger. My husband is too rich. My father is a little bit rich, not too safe for his money, either. If I kill myself, nobody will be left to look after my baby. OK, you are right. I must get a job, a nice job with English. What jobs did you say?"

"You wouldn't like nursing, you'd have to leave the baby."

"No – no nursing."

"University. That would take at least three years to get a profession."

"Too long," Penny said.

"There is secretarial work. You could learn to type and then perhaps find a job in an Embassy with your English. There's also the teaching profession."

She cupped her pretty chin in the palm of her hand, thinking hard. She rubbed her cheek gently; black eyes steel points of concentration.

"The last year in the convent," she remarked, in a tone of speculation, "I was always best in English, better than Sister Benedict. When she went out, I was the teacher. I liked being the teacher. It is very honourable. I taught English with pride – out of class, too."

I signed with relief. "Then be a teacher. This country needs teachers more than any other profession."

Caressing lightly the roundness beneath the peacock silk, Penny envisaged her future with true Chinese sentiment.

"A son could be proud of even a disgraceful mother if she was a teacher, most honourable profession," she answered and jumped to the precarious balance of her feet.

"My father is the one. He will take many hours but he will give in, being surrounded with women. In the end he will be forced to stop me killing myself; Mother crying ever and ever; Aunt Rosy blushing whenever he passes; and all the English class looking upon him with eyes of compassion. I must have six arguments, only three would be no good for his sake."

I did not offer luck, which would have been superfluous.

~

By means of the usual round of activity, time moved in busy hops and jumps from Wednesday to Friday before descending into a melancholy tropical weekend saturated with torrents of accumulated rain. By Sunday, to step outside was voluntary immersion in ankle-deep mud, and to remain indoors a depressing submission to the torrid introspection of headache and heat rash. All is certainly bad, I thought, in agreement with Amy Ling as I rose from a sticky, haunted afternoon rest aggravated by the problem of Penny. For once the charm of the view of the river streaked by light through the breaking indigo clouds failed to cheer me. I had no desire to partake of the afternoon tea heralded by the tinkle of tea-cups in the kitchen. Heat-smothered and oppressed, I bathed and powdered my languid body while my mind, confirming my uselessness, taunted me with thoughts of home. I stepped out into the hall as the doorbell rang.

A muddy boy with a wide impish grin passed across my doorstep a basket of orchids half as high as himself, protected by a dripping cover of loosely woven rattan supported above the flowers on narrow bamboo sticks. Delicate lilac, chiffon white, shell-pink, the fragile sprays glistened like amethyst and silver from the velvet centre where the stalks were embed-ded in moss. The boy who was offering me a rainbow, hovered in the hope of a tip, and gratified beyond his expectation, departed.

Red is the colour of good luck in Chinese and red was splashed on a card attached to a carved ivory fan nestling in the clustered orchid stems. A message was printed in English with the fine swift strokes of a Chinese pen:

"Dear mother of us all and English Teacher

Happy Birthday and Good Luck

From Amy and Penny"

Laughter sparkled in me like the sun on the river. It was the month of May, and my birthday is in September.

THE BARONESS

We were introduced to Marcus Klomp not long after our arrival in Indonesia. Many people in Jakarta seemed to know and respect him, and we heard that he held a safe residence visa from the Independence regime, and that the Indonesians were not of a mind to revoke it. He was the manager of a locally owned firm which imported and re-distributed cotton goods throughout the islands, in minor, undisputed competition with the Chinese who much preferred his business style to that of the Indonesians who distrusted them. He was a single man with an excellent command of languages, and manners along with his natural reserve, which gave him standing as a splendid extra man in an emergency such as a dinner party. Instead of the Curate there was always Marcus, and no hostess stayed long annoyed about a broken coffee cup after she received the sweet apologetic note and the flowers from Marcus the morning after. There seemed to be no doubt that awkwardness was never held against Marcus. On the contrary it seemed to enhance his childlike charm.

One old friend, Jacques, in the French diplomatic service, who was often possessed of a sardonic humour, found this awkwardness highly amusing and made a point of inviting Marcus to the club as the fourth in a game of the strenuous tennis that was supposed to keep foreigners fit in a beastly climate. Marcus would oblige Jacques on these occasions but without enthusiasm, for he was not a sportsman beyond sociability. Usually, he partnered Jacques laconically in a losing game until about match point when, almost invariably, he precipitated an unexpected return from an exasperated French opponent that landed that dignified gentleman on all fours on the court or straddled him across the net. Red-faced and unhappy, Marcus would always apologisze over-profusely and embarrass an often-arrogant Gallic sophistication. Convulsed with inner mirth, Jacques then paid willingly for more than a full round of drinks. No woman with whom I ever sat at the afternoon-tea table had any sympathy for Jacques or whichever of his opponents limped off the court to the bar. We were always embarrassed for Marcus, and Jacques' wife Martine made a point of waylaying this procession and forcing the players to mellow their conversation by downing their Bols at the table of the ladies taking tea. Strangely enough, Marcus made plain his appreciation of Jacques' amusement at his expense, perhaps because only Jacques laughed at him while the rest of us sighed for him. Anyway, it was with Jacques and Martine that we were invited for cocktails at Marcus Klomp's house.

He lived in the best part of the city, on a tree-lined street within walking distance of several embassies, and in a house and garden so small it was immediately evident that he suffered no threat of requisition. Marcus crowded us into a twelve-by-twelve sitting room opening into a six-by-six open courtyard, two sides of which were high brick walls and the other a tiny single bedroom and a four-by-four square Dutch bathroom. There was one other door off the courtyard, which I presumed led to the kitchen, for through it I caught a glimpse of a small hand passing out a plate of savouries. Marcus, with the aid of self-appointed barmen, served the drinks himself, and the food was displayed on the dining table pushed back against the living room wall. Although in such crowded conditions I could scarcely see the details of it, I was charmed with the little house which, in spite of the crowd, seemed tall of ceiling, dignified and cool. Before we got into the car to leave, I looked back and discovered that the house was surrounded on all sides by two-storied mansions of pretentious Dutch colonial architecture. The house on the right, which pressed it almost to the point of over-hanging, was a huge sprawling affair of dilapidated plaster and pillars which, except for a plaque in Bahasa on the gate, gave every appearance of being abandoned.

"Thank goodness we are out of that sardine can," somebody remarked, passing our car. "Old Marcus says he never asks more than thirty to a 'standing room only'; they must have come all at once. I couldn't even see the Baroness!"

"Did you see the Baroness?" I enquired of Jacques as we drove off.

He laughed. "With difficulty, I have turned my back on the Baroness and you do not even see her. Quel domage!"

"Why didn't you introduce me, then?"

"To a painted witch, Cherie – to an oil on the wall?"

"Do you mean the portrait above the table? Is that the Baroness?"

"Oui, that is the Baroness."

"Who is she?"

"Alors, I don't know. There is something, but Marcus does not say. He is, what you say in English, close about his Baroness."

"How long have you known him, Jacques?"

"A year perhaps, perhaps plus, but this is nothing. Everybody knows Marcus, but not intimately, you understand, Cherie."

"What a quaint little house. I didn't see any servants, did you?"

"Non, but is this extraordinaire, when it is so small, the house? I understand he has a maid, just one at a time, never the long time. He is discreet, perhaps, our Marcus."

"Under the eye of his Baroness, perhaps," I countered.

Jacques laughed again. "You are romantique, Cherie, tres, tres romantique – too romantique for the practical arrangements of these islands. Marcus is just a nice boy but without glamour, without mystery. You will see."

"Then how do you account for the Baroness?"

"It is Marcus who must account for the Baroness, and he does not. The portrait he adores, and who can tell a nice boy like that she is bad art. Or who can ask who she is and why such a prominent treasure, without admitting one's dislike. You see, it is all very simple: for the same reason nobody asks, and therefore nobody knows."

The day after Marcus Klomp's party, I had occasion to drive to Tanjung Priok harbour to pick up friends travelling through to Sydney. I remember that while driving down to Priok my mind was still hovering in the house of Marcus Klomp and that I felt uneasily provoked at my inability to recall the features of the Baroness.

After my friends sailed on to Sydney, following their exceptionally rapid tour of Jakarta, both Marcus and the contents of his house escaped my thoughts. I did not even see Marcus for several weeks, and nobody mentioned his name until we made up our list for a small reception. It seemed a nice gesture to invite Marcus in return for his hospitality to us. When he came, his manner was as sweet and ineffectual as a mouth organ in a brass band until he backed into a waiter with a tray full of glasses. The boy was badly cut and afterwards limped around with his leg bandaged up for six weeks.

Poor Marcus; we all felt sorry for him. He was abject in his concern and haunted our telephone with inquiries and apologies. He managed to replace my glasses with finer ones and compensated the boy with a gift. In fact, the consensus held that the catastrophe was really the servant's fault and that, everything considered, it was a wonder how few accidents poor service produced. Only Marcus blamed himself. As a final gesture to make up for the inconvenience he had caused us, he suggested a little dinner at his house, which he would prepare with his own hands. We accepted gracefully, hoping this would be the end of the matter.

At this intimate, exquisitely arranged dinner party, I was seated on Marcus' right facing the portrait of the Baroness. Jacques, I noticed, was facing the little courtyard with his back to the painting. As Marcus made himself unnecessarily busy promoting the appetites of his guests, I had ample opportunity to study the painting, and I did. The portrait, as Jacques had intimated, was disturbing but I could not dismiss this quality as bad art, nor could I agree that the Baroness looked like a witch. The small, heart-shaped face was portrayed in the manner of lesser royalty destined to hang without importance as decoration in a baronial family hall. The mouth was as thin and straight as the eyebrows, and the eyes remote and passionless. The little face, although smooth with resignation, was lacking the lines of age. You could not tell upon what principles the personality functioned, nor did it seem improper to wonder if the face had ever functioned as a human being at all. Perhaps the Baroness was dwarfed by the heavy rococo gold-leaf frame that enclosed her. Inside it she seemed ageless, unfulfilled, spiritless, flat – certainly a strange inspiration for poor Marcus or, for that matter, the artist, whoever he was. Unless, of course, the Baroness was one of those people who could disguise her emotions; hide her feelings from an artist she disliked. Could the reverse also be possible – could a clever artist blank out the emotions of a sitter who displeased him?

I must have stared obviously at the Baroness, for Marcus noticed. But he only spoke to me over coffee when the other guests were absorbed in animated discussion sparked by Jacques at the other end of the table.

"I would give you anything, Madame," Marcus said softly, re-seating himself, "anything to make up for my idiotic blunder, except the portrait of my Baroness, which I see you recognisze as a work of genius."

I jumped and then to recover, sugared my coffee slowly.

"The face is – is most intriguing, Marcus," I replied, and then, in spite of my intentions, asked the question. "Who is the artist?"

"My father," he said, and then looked down at the table with obsequious modesty.

"Then it must be of very great value to you."

"It is indeed – it was finished just before fire destroyed my father's studio."

"But you managed to save it."

"I am afraid, Madame, I was not so heroic. As soon as my father finished the portrait, he ordered me to take it out of his sight. In my enthusiasm I did not realise the portrait was distasteful to him and made the mistake of admiring it."

I looked again at the painting and spoke my thought. "Was it perhaps that your father was not satisfied with his work?"

"I regret that, for me, he was not satisfied with the Baroness, Madame."

I glanced at him quickly to see if he was joking but his gaze upon me was a serious and wide-eyed as a trusting child innocently sharing a cherished confidence. I was caught in one of those anxious moment when silence is infinitely preferable in a situation compelling speech, so my words had to be tentative and questioning.

"The Baroness is not your mother then?"

"Oh no, Madame. My mother died when I was just a boy. We were out riding together. My horse bolted and she came after me and was thrown."

"Oh dear, I'm so sorry, Marcus – I shouldn't have asked. Forgive me."

His smile was full of concern for me. "Pray do not be distressed," he said. "Your question was perfectly natural. It was a tragedy at the time, yes, for she did not want me to learn to ride, nor had I the inclination. My father insisted – he considered the sport manly, you understand, and he was perfectly right, you must agree. Anyway, it happened a long time ago, dear lady, and I have long since recovered."

"You are very kind," I murmured.

"It is you, Madame, who are kind," he said softly, "for you have admired my portrait and I am grateful. The truth is, most guests do not speak of her at all. May I bring you a Cognac?"

As Marcus rose to fill the glasses the company suddenly hushed and I knew that Jacques had swung into another of his animated repertoire of after-dinner stories. I smiled at my husband and then at Martine, and settled back in my chair to listen. I did not glance again at the Baroness, nor did I allow myself to catch the eye of Marcus until we made our farewells and stood on the doorstep ready to depart. As usual, Marcus dismissed the compliments paid to him for a superb dinner with apologies for the service which had, of necessity, been personal.

"She is shy, this new cook I have in my kitchen," he told Martine, "and I find she has much less experience than she led me to believe. I hope she will improve with time."

"Alors, and what happened to the last one you had, Marcus?" Jacques inquired. "You told me she had learned to produce faultless soufflé."

"Alas, my friend, she had a misfortune." Marcus smiled sadly. "She slipped in the mud of the pasar and returned to her kampong to mend her broken arm."

~

Now, I would not like it assumed that I forgo common-sense to operate on intuition but there are times when intuition is common-sense. The degree of difference is subtle but like salt in the stew none the less important. I do not consciously apply an intuitional technique, but on occasion intuition governs me to a point of extraordinary self-preservation by means of an indefinable state of inactivity and mental uncertainty. This condition was particularly unpleasant in an animistic tropical setting that intensifies every hoot of an owl or flight of black bats, let alone the blood-curdling crow of a sacrificial cock near home on the banks of the river. Usually, my intuitional apprehension passes with time or suddenly explodes like a pricked balloon. On rare occasions it focuses on an object or a person. I did not realise, at first, that after his dinner party such a person was Marcus Klomp. In fact, my intention was to make a special effort to remember to be kind to him. Instead, I found myself avoiding him with unpremeditated and unintentional finesse.

I knew why soon after: one sultry oppressive afternoon, when sensible Jakarta citizens slept, there was a ridiculous catastrophe at the club. Four bored little boys with nothing else to do climbed to the roof of the tennis shelter and brought it down to the level of the grass with themselves a screaming mass of arms and legs in the centre of the debris. I was lying restless on my bed when a friend telephoned to tell me that Jacques and Martine's little boy, Gerard, had been knocked on the head and was threatened with concussion. I dressed hurriedly, called a betjak, a means of transport forbidden to me even when all the cars were out, and was precariously pedalled down the main road between honking vehicles. In Jacques' drawing room I waited in anxious company for the doctor to come out of the bedroom with Jacques and Martine. Fortunately, the diagnosis, when it came, was good. Gerard had only been temporarily knocked out and was presently sick in the stomach from shock. The other boys, I was informed, had suffered only cuts and bruises severe enough to keep them away from roofs in the future. All present enjoyed a drink to steady the nerves before Jacques dropped me home on his way to the Embassy. During the drive, Jacques was excited with relief and inclined to witticisms concerning the exploits of small boys. Then suddenly, as we braked in front of my driveway, he threw up his hands and said:

"Alors, and what happened to Marcus?"

"Marcus?" I echoed blankly.

"Didn't you see him? He brought Gerard home."

"No!"

"Quel domage! I did not have a chance to thank him. He pulled all those merchant little beggars out of the wreck. He was the only one close enough to see what happened. Didn't anybody tell you?"

The following week, Marcus, in absentia, dominated conversations given his role as a modest hero. Marcus himself I did not see, for I kept well away from any place where I thought he might be. I felt mean about it, but this did not prevent my shrewd manoeuvres. My strategies were probably unnecessary, because it was remarked that Marcus was very busy preparing for a business trip involving air travel. This news did not relieve my apprehension. On the contrary, I grew irritable and nervy, and made my husband postpone a trip to Singapore. I had, of course, no knowledge of the direction in which Marcus intended to travel, so I made myself a nuisance among my acquaintances with subtle inquiries and warning innuendoes respecting the routes and dates of expectant travellers. Nobody seemed to know or care where Marcus was going, or how soon, but both my husband and Jacques came to the conclusion that the climate was getting me down and suggested I consider a holiday in the cooler altitude of the mountains.

It was Marcus himself who supplied the information about his journey. He arrived one morning during business hours with a large package and a bouquet of orchids. He stood in my living room and bewailed my absence from every location in which he had hoped to see me during the past two weeks.

He had worried, he said, in case he had inadvertently given offence until he had heard I was indisposed.

"The weather perhaps, Madame?" he asked anxiously.

As he stood before me, I was filled with a terrible compassion for his eager eyes, his careful manners, his ingratiating smile, and I hated myself as my feet stood rooted to my own safe carpet and my head shook at his suggestion that we should sit on the balcony. I waved him into a chair on the other side of the room, called the servant to bring us coffee and sat too carefully on a chair a yard away from him. I hoped he did not notice the tremendous effort I made to speak or how my voice trembled.

"It is true I am not myself, Marcus – it might be the weather but I think I may be coming down with something. I'm terribly irritable and jumpy."

"My poor Madame. My apologies for not telephoning. I should not have arrived unannounced like this. Forgive me, I can see you are not yourself, indeed I can. Believe me I came only because time presses. I go this afternoon to Kalimantan. One of our consignments has suffered damage in the unloading."

"Don't go," I heard myself croak bluntly, "Kalimantan isn't safe." He looked surprised and touched.

"You are kind, Madame. You have no doubt heard rumours about the landing fields. I go in a chartered plane and I know the pilot. I trust him absolutely."

"Only one pilot?"

"Only one pilot and myself; it is a very short journey, Madame, and I am grateful, most grateful for your concern. You make my request easier. I admit I wondered about asking Jacques but I feel he does not like the portrait, so I presume upon your kindness since you, of all my guests, admired the Baroness."

"The Baroness?"

"The portrait is here in the parcel in the hope that you will guard it until my return. Since the robbery next door on the night before last, I fear for my treasure as you will understand. May I presume on your kindness? It is only a matter of a few days, a week at the most."

"I – it is a great responsibility," I whispered, aghast.

His pale blue eyes lit up with sympathy. "My poor Madame," he said, "I will go now – you are indeed indisposed. I can hear you have laryngitis by your voice. There is no responsibility, no responsibility at all, Madame. She is, after all, only a portrait, not the Baroness. With you I feel she is safe but if not, it will not matter – we will both have done our best. More we cannot do."

He rose, walked to the door and turned to bow.

"My compliments, Madame, for your immediate return to health. Do not rise, I beg of you. Adieu."

"Thank you for the orchids."

"Indeed, it is my pleasure – a very small appreciation, Madame."

Smiling, he bowed again and like a ghost was gone. Poor Marcus, unlike the rose he did not display the thorn nor even suspect its presence on the stem of his flesh. As a catalyst for precipitating explosive contraction and fragmentation, he bumped into the fatal absurdities floating within range of average existence with wide-open arms and a welcoming smile.

~

Of course, you will know that Marcus did not come back. The pilot was young, only twenty-one years old, and it was said that he lacked experience. You will wonder, no doubt, what I could do to dispose of the portrait of the Baroness and be pleased to hear as I was, that a certain Madame Winklerhof had flown out from Holland to settle the private affairs of Marcus Klomp. There was considerable speculation concerning this lady, for she requested complete privacy out of respect for the deceased and the sadness of her mission. Those people who felt they had known Marcus well for years, a company which naturally excluded both Jacques and myself, agreed that she must be a sister, for letters to Marcus in her handwriting had come regularly for years. Marcus had often given the stamps to one of the secretaries in his office, and this lady verified the script. When I heard of the arrival of Madame Winklehof, I wrote her a short note explaining that I was in possession of a portrait belonging to Marcus that I wished to return. I sent the note through diplomatic channels to the Dutch representative and received a typed note back from the same source to say that Madame Winklehof would expect me to call at the home of the late Marcus Klomp at four o'clock the following afternoon.

The afternoon was heavy with thunderous black clouds that threatened an obliterating downpour at any moment and my driver, for I had made sure of a car, hustled the still-wrapped portrait into the back seat of the car just before the first large drops of rain fell. On the way we had to stop the car and wait until the first deluge ceased. The air was a little cooler as we drew up in front of the little house that had belonged to Marcus, and there was a temporary cessation of the rain. I hurried behind the driver to the shelter of the verandah. The door was open, and I decided to stand the parcel against the wall just inside. The driver went back to the car and I knocked.

"Come in," a voice insisted sharply.

She was sitting on a chair in the middle of the small living room facing the courtyard. I recognised her immediately. There was no need to replace the portrait on the wall behind her. She had the same ageless air and the same blank eyes. She did not rise, although I saw at once she was no older than Marcus. When she spoke, her mouth was tight and bitter and her English clipped but perfect.

"Do sit," she said, "I believe you have brought me a portrait."

"Yes."

"You do not wish to keep it?"

"It is not mine. Marcus brought it to my house to care for until his return."

"Why?"

"He told me the big house next door to this one was recently robbed."

"Indeed. Did he also tell you the house was burned and sacked and is said to be haunted, which no doubt it is, since my husband was murdered in it by the Japanese and his brother with him and his brother's son, since they were too stubborn to leave?"

I was taken aback but only slightly. Her rudeness in refusing to rise had somehow bolstered my intention to deliver the painting and depart as quickly as possible. My answer was cool.

"I would not like you to make the mistake of thinking I knew Marcus Klomp well. I have only been in Jakarta a few months."

"Long enough, if you are perceptive. You know who I am. Marcus trusted you with my portrait. Is it surprising I should assume you also know I owned this house and the one next door before it was requisitioned?"

Suddenly I sensed that this strange woman was jealous, that she had loved Marcus Klomp and was hurt and hurting back.

"All I know," I said gently, "is that Markus valued your portrait more than anything else in the world."

"Did he tell you that?"

"Yes. He told everybody that and nothing else. For that reason, I imagined you were dead."

She looked at me strangely for a moment, but her face showed no emotion that I could recognise.

"I am dead," she said. "I did not die when the Baron died, for my parents arranged the marriage, nor when the ship I escaped in sank, or even when I was picked up by the Japanese and put in a prison camp. I died when I could not marry Marcus, when he burned down his father's house without knowing he did it. I died when I knew how it was with Marcus. Do you know what I am talking about? Do you?"

Slowly, almost imperceptibly, I nodded.

"Marcus did not understand. He thought it was the disapproval of his father. His father – I was a Baroness, his father a penniless artist."

There was no arrogance in her voice, only disdain.

"You see, I met Marcus on the ship that brought us both home from the prison camp. Marcus was kind. Nobody had ever been so kind to me in all my life. We planned to be married the next summer, but all the accidents began to happen, unimportant but happening all the time, one after the other. And finally there was the fire, and even though his father perished in it, Marcus didn't realise. I sent him out here to the Baron's gatehouse and promised I would follow. It was then I died. I should have married Marcus."

"Oh, no," I said, "you couldn't have married him, not with the fear."

For the first time her whole face changed and her blank, pale eyes lit up with a kind of horror.

"Fear!" she snapped. "For you fear, perhaps, because you sensed poor Marcus attracted calamity. But I have been haunted by calamity all my life, disciplined by chaos. I was the one woman to find his strange capacity tenable. Oh no, you do not die of fear. You die of pride."

She paused and, when I made no comment, shrugged.

"Of course, it is not possible for you to understand. You have not endured my upbringing, the perpetuation instinct that drives all before it in a dying aristocracy destined to dig yams for the Japanese. I wanted children. I was unwilling to sacrifice the inheritance of my blood. And I could not have the children of Marcus, not when I knew. So, I sacrificed Marcus and killed myself."

I looked at the bird-like woman whose hard control was such that neither her hands nor feet had moved once during her odd, self-imposed confession. Unexpectedly I felt no pity for her but rather the compassionate benevolence of a priest in the shelter of the sanctuary.

"But you did not sacrifice Marcus," I told her with sudden truth.

"I did. I should have married him. I could have protected him."

"You did protect him. You sent him here, where the Indonesians liked him, and the Chinese gave him respect and he could live on the fringe of a European society that did not demand of him the intimacy he reserved for you in the shadow of your portrait. As a Dutch Baroness you would not have been welcome in this country as his wife, and he would have felt he hurt you. It was you yourself you sacrificed. You know as well as I do that sooner or later he was destined to die with one of those he attracted to calamity, but he was such a nice boy he didn't know."

"A nice boy – did you say nice boy?"

"Yes, that's what everybody called him – a nice boy. Nobody disliked him or was suspicious of him because they did not know him well enough."

"Except you?"

I looked straight into her blank, pale eyes.

"I suffered an intuition – like a bad dream. It can happen to anyone."

Her eyes flickered for the first time and fell.

"Forgive me," she whispered, "you are right. It can happen to anyone. It would have happened over and over again in Europe without the exoneration of voodoo. Thank you for telling me he did not know."

She raised her eyes again and slowly, terribly, they began to shimmer with tears. She tried to speak and her voice choked on her words, but I heard her as distinctly as the fall of the portrait in the hall.

"He didn't change. He didn't know. He died an innocent, as innocent as the child I never had." Her hands, smooth in her lap rose to receive her face.

I left the room quietly and picked up the parcelled portrait to lean it back against the wall before I went out into the gusty wind that heralded another downpour of tropical rain.

THE BLUE OF
THE SKY

Veni was born in Semarang of a Sundanese-Dutch father
and a Balinese-Dutch mother. By the time of her birth, both
her Dutch grandfathers were dead many years but unforgotten
in her paternal grandmother's house and its spacious walled
garden behind the family business, which was the manufac-
ture of cork-soled sandals of infinite variety and charm. When
Veni's father married, his new wife's mother was already a
widow and came to live on these premises with her daughter,
which was an amicable arrangement as both grandmothers
were said to have that superior feeling of being the widows
of Dutch husbands and got along well together. In fact, the
marriage of their children was negotiated at their instigation.
Both took an interest and worked in the shoe factory in some
capacity but Veni's father was rightly accepted as the manager
as he had inherited not only his Dutch father's light eyes, but
also his business acumen. The arrival of little Veni as second
daughter to the household was taken as an omen of joy, for
unlike her elder sister, her eyes changed to the blue of the
sky instead of remaining dark and were a source of wonder in
her small-boned oval face, a feature that wiped out disappointment that she was not a son. Her parents were very young
and extraordinarily handsome, and time and genuine affection
were in their favour.

As a baby, Veni was very spoiled and never allowed to crawl or cry. The two grandmothers, the servants, and all the female factory hands rushed to lift her in their arms if she so much as squeaked. But as soon as she learned to walk her sister taught her to play, which she much preferred, and to hide when eager arms sought to show her off to customers buying shoes. Since even her naughtiness was a delight to her elders, Veni was a very happy child.

However, when she was two years old a tragedy descended on her elders. Her mother, who had grown up in Surakarta destined to become a court dancer chosen for the Legong as a child, and trained in the Kraton to distinguish herself in the Bedojo in the Palace of the Sultan, died suddenly of fever in the fourth month of her third pregnancy. Both grandmothers neglected Veni and went into deep mourning with constant lamentation; the maternal grandmother for her exquisite daughter and the paternal grandmother for the grandson and blue-eyed heir she was certain she had lost with the bereavement. There descended on the beautiful garden in which Veni played with her sister, a gloom unalleviated by any superstitious comfort nor the ministrations of potions offered from kampongs as far away as the outskirts of Batavia and Den Pasar. It was evident a curse had fallen on the weeping grandmothers, which sooner or later would extinguish them. The shoe shop was over-run with tukangs demanding large sums of money for cures, and those dismissed without trial threatened the management and frightened the customers. Veni's father was driven to distraction and, to settle the issue, decided to take another wife and if necessary two, in order to produce a son and get on with the shoe business.

This momentous decision was made six months after the death of Veni's mother and satisfied the paternal grandmother, who stopped weeping and sent for a marriage broker with the hope of finding another candidate with suitable prestige to become the wife of a successful factory owner with blue eyes.

The maternal grandmother, however, was visited in the night by her departed daughter in the guise of a fluttering bird, weeping in distress. So she threatened the paternal grandmother that the powers of evil would descend on her household if her son took another wife. In return, the paternal grandmother who was, after all, the head of the family, ordered the maternal grandmother out of the house – although her son protested and Veni cried because her elder sister cried. It was a miserable situation and Veni's father felt very upset about it as he mourned his wife with a greater grief than any new wife would compensate. As a kind of fee of retribution, he found a tiny house in a village in the countryside and supported his mother-in-law there with a servant called Iam, of whom she was fond, where he promised to come with her granddaughters for a visit once every six months. It was the best he could do as his mother opposed him and he was forced to allow her full choice of the new wife.

Veni was too small to miss her mother and her maternal grandmother, but not too small to aggravate her father's new wife, who produced three little girls in three years, all of whom had black eyes. The paternal grandmother had taken her time and used her discretion and even delayed her choice of a second wife long enough to find a girl of Sundanese parentage like herself, equally strong in constitution and possessed of a Dutch grandparent. Her disappointment in the new progeny was acute, and after the birth of the second black-eyed baby girl, her attention swung back to Veni, who was as pretty as a doll and as smart as an owl. Veni was given dancing lessons and taught to read and write in Dutch as a prelude to attendance at a Catholic convent school that offered the opportunity of higher education to girls of mixed race. When she was accepted at the convent, Veni refused to enter without her sister, who was her loving protector against the subtle minor cruelties of her father's new wife. Fortunately, both the girls were satisfactorily established as weekly pupils at the convent by the time the fourth baby arrived. This one was black-eyed as usual, but a son.

The convent, like any other hoped-for but unexpected gift, held for Veni's sister an attraction that Veni herself never quite understood, although she realised vaguely that her sister was old enough to adore her mother and subsequently hate her replacement. Adek had also been long enough in the local overcrowded primary school to appreciate the different degree of respect you received if you went to school with Dutch girls. The nuns would not allow obvious distinction within the school, and Adek realised they practised loving-kindness with a severity past normal common-sense in respect to girls like herself and Veni. As at home, Adek basked in the reflected light of Veni without any feeling other than pride. She was not in the least surprised that the older Dutch girls and the nuns should fuss over Veni, who was tiny as a fairy, clever and had blue eyes. The big girls would persuade Veni to dance when the nuns were absent. It all seemed perfectly natural to Adek who was there, according to their father's own words, to look after Veni.

Veni did not appreciate the privilege of the convent, or the Dutch language, or the attention lavished on her, except as a relief from her stepmother. She had liked the dancing lessons best. But her grandmother said she had to learn because she had blue eyes. Most of the girls in the convent had blue eyes, so the remark made sense to Veni and she had Adek, whom she could not do without. After the birth of the new baby boy, the celebrations were long and overcrowded with her stepmother's relatives, such that her paternal grandmother shifted her concentration. Adek told Veni she thought she should work for a prize to justify their placing in the school until the fuss died down. Veni did. She started with the singing prize, endowed as she was with rhythm, a high, clear, bell-like voice, and the appearance of a little angel in her high-necked white pinafore, singing the hymns. At the end of the first year she also won the class certificate for proficiency, for she had sat under her grandmother's eye learning from a private tutor for the whole of the previous year. She received a tremendous ovation at the prize-giving since her Balinese bone structure, in comparison to the average height of other children of seven gave her the air of a child prodigy, which the good Sisters were convinced she was, and for which reason made sure Adek received a prize as well. The Mother Superior was loath to see Veni depart for the vacation. The presence of a little girl like Veni alleviated the terrible pain in the hearts of all the nuns. Holland had just been conquered and occupied by the Germans.

In the house behind the sandal factory, all traces of cele-bration were removed and all the relatives of the second wife departed except for an elderly blind aunt who remained to be kept as compensation for the abrupt ending of festivities. This woman, sharp-tongued and longing bitterly for her Cheribon kampong, sat all day in the garden in the company of the nursemaid and children of the second wife. Adek and Veni were established in new sleeping quarters in a small anteroom in the apartments of their paternal grandmother, instead of in the house of their father where their room was now the nursery of the son and heir. Almost at once they were put to work in the factory, sorting material for the strappings and running errands for the women. As they lay on their mats in the dark of night, Adek told Veni that something was wrong with the house, that the workers were not happy and hated grandmother and the second wife. Veni had better do every-thing she could to be useful and popular in the shoe shop and make up to her new baby brother who was now the first importance in the house. To please Adek, Veni said she would.

She did not mind working in the shop for the short period of the holiday before she returned to the convent, which she now preferred to home. She made a game of studying all the feet in the shop and deciding which could dance and which could not. It made her capable of picking a style and a size for a customer with such precise and charming innocence that her choice was allowed. But no more packages of sandals were being dispatched to Holland, and deliveries to the homes of the rich had declined to a trickle. It took her father, with the uninvited and insistent collaboration of his wife and mother, no more than an hour every morning to add up the orders for the day. During this time Veni danced in the garden under the encouragement of small sisters and servants but mainly for the benefit of her baby brother who clapped his pudgy dimpled hands in glee, sitting up in his basket. There was no mention of a visit to the country house of their maternal grandmother until one afternoon a week before classes were due to commence. On this day the servant of the maternal grandmother arrived to inquire why no letter had come. Maternal grandmother was perturbed. She had not seen her granddaughters for a year, having politely and courteously refrained from expecting the promised visit during the celebrations in honour of the deceased daughter's husband's much-welcomed son. The paternal grandmother and the second wife were furious when the servant Iam refused to depart intimidated after their combined tongue-lashing and insisted on a final word from the master. Veni's father, harassed past endurance by the two women, and perhaps remembering happier days with his first wife in his garden, decided against his wife and mother, granting the servant three days to take Adek and Veni to present their respects to maternal grandmother.

The journey was made on a cart drawn by an ox that belonged to the recently acquired husband of the servant Iam. This box-like vehicle was waiting outside the street entrance to the sandal factory where the great white ox was much admired and the owner congratulated on his wit at the expense of certain white-skinned masters who had suffered a body-blow to their prestige by others of their warlike, pale-skinned species. This amusing man who was doubtless an illiterate peasant with no idea where Europe was, said it was in flames and for all he cared could burn to the ground. The workers in the shoe factory in the absence of the master, stood in the doorway and joined the passers-by in the street to laugh at the country bumpkin's excruciatingly funny sallies.

The father of the two little girls would not allow them to travel by night, so a start was arranged two hours after dawn on the following morning. The servant and her husband were instructed to take the children by the most direct route – by ox-cart a journey calculated by Veni's father to take about eight hours, allowing a mid-day rest for the comfort of the ox. Under no circumstances were the little girls to arrive or depart their maternal grandmother's house in the hours of darkness. This was the first time the father of Veni and Adek had not accompanied the children by bus or hired a car himself, and the servant accepted her responsibility in the full knowledge that the livelihood of herself and the maternal grandmother depended on her.

To Veni it was the most memorable journey she had undertaken in her short life. The ox-cart was very old and rigged with a high-peaked and plaited rattan cover that swept like guardian garuda wings between its sheltered passengers and the sun. The servant and her husband re-arranged the inside of the cart in which they had spent the night, swept it free of straw and filled two sacks full of fresh chaff upon which they piled woven mats so the little girls, particularly Veni, could sit high enough to see the countryside as they rode along. A large basket of fruits and a metal container of Chinese origin protecting the lunch were tucked in beside their bundles. A tremendous excitement filled Veni's heart as they lumbered through the crowded streets of Semarang and beyond the shaggy green banana groves and rice paddies along the country road that ultimately led to Surakarta. Veni was so happy she began to sing.

The owner of the ox-cart, who was the husband of the servant of maternal grandmother, was not only a country yckel possessed of wit with an ignorant political twist but also a performer of Wayang shadow plays and a beater of the gong in the gamelan. When he heard Veni sing, he was delighted and he put his heart and the whole range of an enormous voice into chanting with her. The journey was a joy from beginning to end. When the singing waned, the driver of the cart spoke the tales of Arjuna, the white prince of the Wayang, and Veni knew all the stories from her dancing lessons and her little fingers mimed the movements as she sat on the high sacks expecting the monkey god to jump out at her from a bursting kapok pod hanging over the road on the branch of its twisted tree.

Some time before noon, the ox-cart swung off the main road to Surakarta and by-passed it on a lesser road that led through the very centre of a village where the market was in full swing. The great ox relaxed his laborious plod and turned his head toward the green grass at the edge of the village square where the platform stood. It was obvious that the ox had visited this village before and expected to rest in the shade of the pavilion. The driver of the ox-cart jumped from the high seat beside his wife and reached into the back to lift Veni in his arms while his wife helped Adek. They went, all four, into the market and walked up and down looking at the piles of baskets, mats, pots and hats; the magnificent bright colours of batiks and kain spread out on display; at the food trays of spices, dried fish and rice cakes; at the eggs, green vegetables, fruit and bottled sugar drinks. Everywhere the lean, brown driver of the ox-cart was recognised with laughter and feted. He lifted Veni in his arms and told all the people she was a Balinese princess, a blue-eyed magic bird of Arjuna, and the people offered her gifts, a fan, a banana and a durian, a humming-bird's tail feather, a coconut and flowers for her hair. She gave the gifts to Adek to hold and sat on the strong shoulders of the ox-driver, who was called Bapa wherever he went, which was very odd since he was nobody's father, really, and certainly not the father of maternal grandmother's servant Iam, who lovingly called him Bapa too.

It seemed very strange to Veni that when she arrived at her grandmother's house, she did not remember it at all, not even that its size was only one sleeping room larger than most of the little houses along the roadside. Nor had she noticed before that maternal grandmother's big room was filled with beautiful objects that must have been displayed in her sitting room in the family house behind the shoe factory. Veni, standing in the middle of this room, was shocked to have overlooked the masks of stark white Arjuna and masks of all his enemies and cohorts that rode with him on the wind of time. She touched gently the sculptured design of the sirih boxes and polished wooden dancing figures on the carved teak tables, and was overwhelmed to sit on the mat in such a room to offer the small oleh-oleh that she and Adek had brought to maternal grandmother.

Also, which was terrifying, she felt she was seeing her maternal grandmother for the first time as she really was, so tiny and slight that Adek, who was by far the shortest girl of nine years at the convent school, was already equally tall and larger of foot. Maternal grandmother was like a frail wizened bird with forever-folded wings and bright black penetrating eyes that permitted no secrets and knew everything there was to know in the whole wide world. It did not matter that maternal grandmother was gentle and kind and moved with no more effort than a little breeze, offering every comfort and benevolence her love could bestow on her granddaughters. Her eyes had looked at Veni and in them the child had seen herself and her own truth; a reflection of her own image, even the size and shape and spirit. It was too much for Veni after such an exciting day, and she forgot that a dancer must have an emotionless face and wept. Maternal grandmother was not disturbed. She took Veni in her arms and crooned a Balinese lullaby her mind had long forgotten. Adek sat and watched, recognised the ancient source that moved them and felt she would have to protect them for as long as both of them lived.

All the village welcomed the children of the child of maternal grandmother for, as Bapa told them, the blue-eyed one would fulfil the music of the dance to be heard in the running of the waters and the living spirit of the trees. In the village square the gamelan was set up in the pavilion on the next night. And Veni heard the music speak with all the melancholy hopes and fears that live in the heart of nature and haunt the heart of man. Bapa beat the great copper drum and, when he wished, silenced it and recited the legend in his loud, penetrating voice. Little Veni sat up nearly all night and once she danced. Not a muscle on her little face showed emotion. Only her fingers fluttered like butterflies at play above the flowers in the grass, and her swaying body responded to the rhythm of the gamelan like the river answers the call of the sea.

Bapa carried Veni back to maternal grandmother's house and later spoke his mind when the children slept behind the screen in the small bedroom.

"Who are these warring fair-skinned ones who hold a child of the gods in the school of the religion of Europa? What right have they? The spirits of the earth beneath the rice will put a curse on them."

"They are the heritage of her blue eyes and our future, Bapa," maternal grandmother replied. "But do not fill your mind with wrath against them. Some, like the father of my child, are filled with goodness and the wisdom taught in their schools is very great."

"The child should go like her mother to the Kraton. The day would come when she might dance the Ketawang Bedojo in honour of the goddess of the sea. I am an ignorant man with no learning, or I would take her there myself."

He stopped to laugh at the folly of this thought and added: "With your permission, of course, Grandmother."

"Do not decry your lack of book-learning, Bapa. Your knowledge is also great and a source of pride to this village. One day you will become a famous dalang. Do not sour your generous soul against the Dutch, Bapa. I have found them kind."

"The talk rises in the kampongs, Grandmother, that their cities burn from the sky. It is said we are their slaves and if we do not fight for freedom, our country will burn too and give us a new set of masters. Surely there is enough of the kris in our souls without that? Will the child return?"

"It is promised she will return, but the new son of her father adds pressure against it, as your wife Iam has told you. Make the return journey swift, Bapa, as the master requested, and do not speak rashly of his ancestors."

There was no joy in the return of Veni and Adek to their father's house in Semarang, for they were received as if they had merely spent the usual week at school and no inquiries were made or enthusiasms expected regarding the journey to the country. Only at the moment of their arrival did their father receive the respects of the maternal grandmother, and even then with interruptions from paternal grandmother and his wife. The factory workers had no opportunity to enjoy the witticism of Bapa, and the minds of the house servants had been poisoned against Iam, who had taken a country yokel for a husband, so that no hospitality was offered when she returned with the children. Almost immediately it was ordered by paternal grandmother that Adek and Veni ask the cook for their supper and retire for rest as their services would be needed as usual early in the morning. It seemed very strange to Veni to lie again beside Adek in the room in paternal grand-mother's large apartment. She felt as if she had wakened in the night from a beautiful dream. Adek whispered that they must remember to do everything exactly the same as they had before the journey and say nothing about their unexpected happiness.

Veni did as Adek suggested, but she felt lonely even with Adek beside her in the big house and shop, and looked with the suspicion of new insight at the strained pale eyes in her father's dark face and the fanatical obsession of her paternal grandmother carrying the grandson in her arms. Noticing as she would never have noticed before the atmosphere around her, she recognised the cunning, satisfied expression on the lips of her stepmother on the big day before the new school term began, so that when her paternal grandmother said that business losses had removed the possibility of a return to the convent, she was not surprised. She felt no more than an expected distaste for the words of paternal grandmother and her eyes, like clear blue glass, stared at her grandmother's face without emotion. Adek was reprimanded sharply because she wept. Veni knew Adek was not weeping for herself.

It was a full week before the Mother Superior came into the shop like a prow in full sail before a high wind, and asked for private words with the master. The paternal grandmother wilted before her, the light blazing in her eyes, and the second wife stared sullenly when she heard the order that sent Veni and Adek out to the garden to play with the younger children. The Mother Superior was closeted a long time with the master, who in her view was the son of an honest Dutchman who had spent the best years of his life in unselfish service to Java. She considered the intellectual capacity already exhibited by Veni the result of her European heritage. As for the financial difficulties faced by the owner of the sandal factory, how could they compare with the financial problems of running a convent when the homeland was bleeding under enemy occupation?

In the back garden, Veni whispered to Adek who was crying again. "I won't go without you. I never go anywhere without you. If we do not go back to the convent, it is certain we will be sent away from here and there is nowhere else to send us except to maternal grandmother, who knows I will dance. You will see. I will not go without you. Don't cry."

~

They did not go to the country but back to the convent, where the food deteriorated but not the lessons. Another Christmas came and Veni sang "Malam kudus, sunji senjap,"–"Silent night, holy night"– in a white dress, and everybody in the audience, remembering their childhood in Holland, felt their eyes swim with tears. The sweet, sad hymn reminded Veni of the gamelan and Bapa booming the melancholy copper gong, which he said had been fashioned in Semarang right under the noses of the ruling ones who did not even know the words it spoke to the people. Not that Veni had time to think very much about the words of Bapa. She was treated like a little princess at the convent, the doll of the pale Dutch girls for whom she danced in secret, and the sustained justification of the teaching Sisters labouring under the mounting threat of a violent freedom revolution, encouraged by the total war in Europe. The nuns taught Veni all they could with delicate restraint of their missionary zeal, for she and Adek were almost the only Indonesian children left whose parents were not converts. Veni, who learned to read and write in Dutch, converse in French with Sister Madelaine, and in Irish-English with Sister Patrick, questioned nothing. She adored Sister Patrick, who was full of fun and young and whose merry eyes overlooked the sin of dancing in the tiny one who was under her care in the dormitory after lessons were finished for the day.

Only once did Sister Patrick feel moved to ask Veni if she had heard the voice of God, and she reported to her superiors the answer she received with awe and satisfaction bordering on thanksgiving.

"God is in the trees and the river and the sea," Veni said, "and his voice speaks out like thunder in the big gong."

The Mother Superior sighed and stored this comment of her most promising pupil at the back of her mind. She did not, at that time, enlighten Sister Patrick who was inexperienced and new to the work of the order in the Dutch East Indies. Instead, she visited the shoe factory to arrange that the father be relieved of the responsibility of the children on the weekends, and offered magnanimously to make a vacation place for them as well, for the purpose of learning embroidery and music.

The father of Veni and Adek, expecting daily the advent of another child to be fed in his garden, regarded the Mother Superior out of narrow, pale eyes, oddly out of place in the brown Sundanese-boned face above his lean, thinly muscled limbs. Soon he would have to decide which Indonesian political party he must join towards the defeat of the oppressor. He was not a Christian and he was not a Muslim, nor was he an illiterate peasant to place offerings under an ancient tree. The brothers of his wife, who were businessmen like himself in Cheribon, had secretly joined the Communist Party of the Indies, the P.K.I., which had been outlawed but was still strong. He was under pressure on behalf of his son and heir, who, like his mother and his grandmother, was a black-eyed Sundanese Indonesian boy who did not show a trace of Dutch ancestry. Once, it seemed to Veni's father now a forgotten time, he had been briefly happy as a handsome youth in the arms of a beautiful bride and the master of a thriving business, bought by a Dutch father he did not know as compensation for the devotion of his mother who had nurtured the heritage carefully to place in the hands of her son. The business was no longer thriving, the patronage of the master-race no longer worth his calculation; the recriminations of his mother a daily trial; the exhortations of his wife's family increasingly persistent that he reject the stigma of his Dutch connection; the voice of his wife insistent that, as soon as possible, he call in the marriage broker for his elder daughters.

The father of Adek and Veni did not reveal this thought to the Mother Superior nor was he able to tell her what he did not realise himself: that he had not loved since death stole his first wife who had been a Balinese dancer. Adek was ten years old, but not, as yet, quite tall enough to prepare for marriage, he said, and Veni, of course, was not yet nine and very small. If the Mother Superior felt able to support the girls at the convent, he was willing that they stay, but she could see for herself that he could not afford to pay. Already his house and business premises were showing signs of dilapidation, and his work-staff had been reduced from twenty satisfied employees to a mere disgruntled seven. His wife was constantly on his back to consider his other children, particularly his son, whom she threatened to send to her family in Cheribon. To save her dignity, the Mother Superior agreed in shocked consternation, and returned to the convent. She felt it her duty to relate her experience to the Sisters under her guidance as a warning against the greater trials she felt they would soon face. Her observant eyes had not missed the outlawed P.K.I. sign scratched on the wall of the shoe factory. The kind, simple face of Sister Patrick clouded with fear for Veni, and she wept.

The father of Adek and Veni, for his part, felt grateful relief at the success of a manoeuvre that temporarily removed one of the burdens from his overloaded shoulders. He was not without strong family feeling, and responsibility for all his children weighed on his conscience. He recognised that the thought of the blue of Veni's eyes filled him with unresolved guilt, for he suspected, not without reason, that she was not an ordinary child.

On occasion he reprimanded himself for not providing that Adek and Veni live with their Balinese grandmother, for whom he retained part of the affection he had lavished on her daughter. But this alternative to the convent no longer existed. for he had been forced to discontinue the allowance sent to the maternal grandmother as compensation to his wife's family for the departure back to Cheribon of the blind aunt who had sat in discontent in his garden. He felt no doubt that Adek and Veni would be safe at the convent until they were of an age to be married. He had done his best for them, and perhaps a little more than might have been expected under his circumstances. He had not failed to observe a greater significance than the Mother Superior in the sign printed in the night on the wall of his premises and had taken to wearing dark glasses. Even so, there was only one more Christmas at the convent for Veni to sing her favourite carol and receive the Christmas proficiency prize in the form of a tiny Bible in a little silver box to wear on a chain around her neck. It was a miserable festive season. No amount of effort on the part of Sister Patrick and Sister Madeleine and the Mother Superior could over-ride the foreboding that had filtered in through the convent gate with the persuasive terror that constant rumour inflicts upon the helplessly trapped.

Two months later the imperial army of Japan landed in Java to "liberate" the Indonesian people from white colonial oppression and offer them Asian co-prosperity under their own leaders returned from Dutch-imposed exile. All over Java, the Dutch and the Indonesians geared themselves for an expected battle. But the Dutch Commander-in-Chief who was also the head of the Allied Forces based in Batavia almost immediately surrendered.

There began a great exodus and movement of people. Dutch and European women and children were rushed away on any available transport until transport was no longer available. Indonesian political agitators took to the mountains, peasants who worked for the Dutch deserted them and returned to their villages. City people searched for shelter in the countryside and the rich Chinese merchants buried their treasures and fled their homes.

When there was no more transport, grim fear descended and those who were left closed their businesses and waited. At the convent the Mother Superior, who had received no instruction, waited. Most of her pupils had returned to the protection of their parents. Some for whom she prayed were on the high seas in the path of Japanese submarines, others cowered on the overcrowded roads to the seaports. Some, with their parents, were trying to forget they were Christians and some that they were both Christian and Chinese. Unexpectedly, the father of Adek and Veni did not come to claim his daughters. The Mother Superior knew that the least she had to face was internment and sent a faithful servant to the shoe shop, which was found to be boarded up and deserted. When the Mother Superior and Sister Patrick told Adek and Veni, Adek cried bitterly but Veni spoke calmly, with her blue eyes on the stricken face of Sister Patrick.

"We will be safe. Maternal grandmother will send Bapa for me and I will take Adek and go in the cart behind the ox."

But in the night, when all was quiet, Adek left her bed and slipped into the bed of Veni and whispered that Bapa would go to the house and find it boarded up and not know where to find them, for he had never been to the convent and neither had Grandmother or Iam or anybody from the village who would know the way. And they couldn't stay in the convent because the Sisters were going away to a place that the enemy said was only for people with white faces, and were afraid for

Veni because it was much better if little girls were kept out of the sight of the enemy. So Veni told Adek to go to sleep and in the morning they would leave the convent and walk at the side of the road to the market village where the ox rested and the people would remember that Bapa had called her a blue-eyed magic bird of Arjuna and go to tell Bapa that she was waiting there.

The Mother Superior and most of the nuns prayed all night in the chapel and the Sisters on duty prayed in their rostered places. Shortly after dawn, a frightened congregation of committed Christians whose skins were blended every shade of white and brown; of Portuguese, Chinese, Indian, Javanese, Sundanese, Malay and Dutch heritage, began to pour into the sanctuary behind the convent gates. All had heard the rumour that the day had come.

Adek and Veni were unable to attract the attention of Sister Patrick, or Sister Madeleine or the Mother Superior, because they had dressed in their only going-home garments of cotton batik instead of the school pinafore. So Veni wrote a note and pinned it on her bed and led her weeping sister to the convent kitchen to ask the cook for a rice cake to put in their bundles. The cook had delayed as long as she could under the angry eye of her son who was waiting impatiently with a betjak hidden in the shrubs at the back gate to take her home where she belonged. When Adek and Veni slipped in the door, she was alone in the bare scrubbed kitchen block, helping herself to the necessities for her journey and was not pleased to see them.

"What permission have you to go?" she demanded.

"We have told the Mother Superior and Sister Patrick," Veni said, "and they do not think it is wise for the enemy to see little girls without their parents here."

"And where do you plan to go?"

"To a market village off the road to Surakarta, three hours by ox-cart where Bapa will be waiting to take us to the village of our maternal grandmother."

The cook mumbled to herself, agitated and unsure about the little girls but in full knowledge of the temper of her son.

"My son waits to take me to my village in the mountains near Salitiga," she muttered at last. "We start in the same direction. Put those rice cakes and bananas in your bundles and come with me to ask if he will take you as well. But if you are seen, we are lost."

The son raged under his breath when he saw the children his mother had brought.

"Do you think I am an ox. Why didn't you hurry? The weight of them will break my back on the rough side tracks we must take all the way now since none of the main roads are safe."

But he did not deny the children as he wheeled the betjak into the lane and mounted his high seat behind and started off. Adek hesitated but Veni pushed her in beside the cook and hopped up herself like a squirrel. Neither of them recognised the alley they traversed through the heart of the town, nor the narrow canal at the edge of the last kampong where a dusty track meandered between rice paddies. The sun rose higher and the heat increased and it seemed as if they would never reach the distant outline of trees that guarded a river. When they reached the river the betjak driver rode straight in through the scrub to the water's edge and threw his sweating body on the ground. His breath like a bellows croaked gradually still before he slithered into the river, splashed like a water-rat, climbed out again and demanded that his mother give him food.

Veni asked, "What is the name of this river?"

"It is the Tuntang. From here on we can follow it more or less all the way to my village."

"Is it near the road to Surakarta?"

"No, why should it be? I am going to my village, not Surakarta."

"We would like to go to a market village off the road to Surakarta."

He bit hungrily into the rice cakes of the convent and answered with his mouth full. "Then why did you get into my betjak? My betjak is going to my village. It is enough that I carry your weight without your complaints."

"There is room enough in our village," the cook said kindly. "Get in the betjak."

They rode along the path that bordered the river. But they had not gone very far when they heard the reverberating sound of the big gong. The betjak driver ran his vehicle off the road behind a big clump of bamboo and told his mother to get out and the girls to stay in.

"There is news," he said, pulling his mother out of the hearing of anxious ears. "The gong is summoning the village. Further up, the road water is diverted into the desa across this road. There is a bridge. We must go down to hear what they say."

"You go," the cook said. "I will look after the girls."

"No. You must put the fear of death into them to sit still. I will take you down and you must creep close. It is there I stole the betjak. It is useless to look shocked. I had no other way to come for you. If you want to take them with you, do as I say. Tell them you think there are bandits in the village."

After the cook and her son had disappeared, Veni told Adek to take her bundle and get out of the betjak without making a sound because they were going to hide.

"I heard the big gong speak," she said, "and it did not warn that bandits were in the village. It was calling people together to tell them something good like Bapa did. The betjak driver is not a good man and I do not want to go to his village, which is not on the road to Surakarta."

"But they will look for us and perhaps we will be beaten for hiding."

"They will not look for us for he does not want us," Veni said.

From their hiding place further back in the bamboo grove, they watched the cook and her son return to the betjak, wheel it out while they argued, saw the man mount the saddle and the woman reluctantly climb in. Then Veni and Adek ate a rice-cake out of their bundle and two bananas to lighten the load they had to carry and set out to find the village of the big gong. When they came to the bridge, they looked down the water-diversion canal and saw a little path beside it winding in and out of the banana plantations. Veni felt no nervousness at all and they ran down the path to the outskirts of the village where a group of small children gaped at them open-mouthed.

"Where is the big gong?" Veni asked.

"You are not allowed to go," a naked little boy replied. "It is not yet time for the Wayang."

And he looked straight in the direction of Veni's back. So she laughed and turned face about and ran again until she came to a break in the houses and saw the pavilion for the gamelan and the square full of groups of people talking with subdued excitement and awe. Nobody took any notice of Veni and Adek until they reached the pavilion that held the big gong. Then suddenly she and Adek were seized by the arm and stopped.

"I want to see the dalang that beats the big gong," Veni cried.

An old man rose from his seat on the ground in front of the pavilion steps. "Well then, here I am," he said, and the people stood back for him while others closed into a circle all around.

Veni bowed and smiled up into the old man's face. "I am Veni," she said, "the daughter of a Balinese dancer, and I am looking for Bapa who calls me the blue-eyed bird of Arjuna. This is my sister who is always with me."

The old dalang did not show his surprise but simply asked, "Where have you come from?"

"From Semarang this morning."

"How did you come?"

"In a betjak along the river. The driver was going to his village, which is not near the road to Surakarta where we wished to go to find Bapa in the market village where he will wait."

A great murmur of voices rose around her, but the dalang held up his hand for silence.

"The road to Surakarta is not open, little one. How is it you have come here?"

"We escaped from the betjak driver and hid from his eyes after I heard the great gong speak and knew we must come here."

"What did the great gong say, little one?"

"That you are good and would take us to Bapa who waits with his cart behind the ox for a journey to our maternal grandmother."

"How is it you did not wait behind closed doors for Bapa?"

"The Holy Sisters were in fear that the eyes of the enemy would find us."

The old man pursed his lips. "All that is spoken is not true," he said slowly. "Some of each race are good and we have yet to feel the goodness of the new freedom we are promised. Are you tired, little one?"

Veni shook her head and looked up at the dalang, still smiling. "But Adek is," she said. "She did not know we were coming to you."

"It is true your eyes hold the blue of the sky," he murmured and added aloud for all to hear. "You are not unwelcome. What is the name of this market village you wish to find?"

"I do not know. I have been there only once. We left Semarang in the ox-cart two hours after dawn and came by order of my father by the most direct route, which was the road to

Surakarta. In the hour before noon, we turned off the main road and came soon to the shade of the village pavilion in the green oval where the ox knew to rest. There were none in the market, which was very rich, who did not know and laugh with Bapa."

A youth pushed forward and addressed Veni. "Is the ox full of years and white?"

"Yes," Veni said.

"And is the Bapa you seek loud with the words of wit and the tales of the Wayang?"

"He speaks the Wayang with the voice of thunder and beats the big gong of the gamelan."

The youth turned to the dalang and said: "I have seen the man of whom she speaks. There could be no other the same, going to Semerang in search of a girl who will dance in the Kraton."

"Will you dance in the Kraton?" the dalang asked Veni.

"Yes," she said. "I will dance."

"Where is this man?" the dalang asked the youth.

"With your permission I will go where I saw him in a small desa this side of the Surakarta road. If he has gone, he may pass again on his return, for none from the villages will use the Surakarta road."

"We have been ordered to go no further than our own rice fields."

The youth bowed his head in deference to the dalang. "I will go with the dusk and return to sleep in the house of my father."

Adek and Veni were given food and taken to the house of the dalang to rest. Adek spoke with emotion of the bravery of the youth and Veni remembered the eyes of the betjak driver and thought of the dalang with gratitude for his goodness.

The daughter of the dalang roused them in the morning with coconut milk in a bowl. The smile of the daughter of the dalang was wide and friendly and she pointed with excitement through the open door, to the green across the square where the white ox rested after his night's journey. And Veni ran and was swept up into the arms of Bapa.

"It is seven days since the bird appeared in the dreams of your maternal grandmother and she sent me to the house of your father to persuade him to let you leave school of the oppressor, which is no longer safe."

"I knew you would come, Bapa."

"Seven days, and five of them spent questioning in the region of your father's closed house."

"Did you find my father, Bapa?"

"I found that there was a moment in the house of your father that shook the souls of all beneath the roof. In the light of day his life was threatened before his workers, and their lives were threatened also, since they worked with one whose sympathy was with the oppressors. That night your paternal grandmother folded her wings and died. When the days of the funeral passed, the period due for respect, your father made his balance and his debts outweighed the resources of his inheritance.

"But, Bapa, why did my father not send for us?"

"Would he hand you to the marriage broker in the presence of his wife's family? His veins, like the blood of your maternal grandmother, ran with trust in the strength and wisdom of the oppressors. He left you where he thought you were safe. He did not live in the village in the truth of the voice of the great gong, but he will hear it now in the mountains, and so will his son."

"Did my father go to the mountains, Bapa?"

"After his accounting, your father distributed the goods in his shop to the workers, bid his wife return to Cheribon, took his son in his arms and closed the door behind him. There is room for all in the mountains."

"Will my father return, Baba?"

"One day he will return to the village of your maternal grandmother, and I will tell him Veni dances where her blue eyes are safe in the Kraton. The new conquerors will respect the Kraton, for it is said the roots of their culture are like our roots and buried deep in the soil of their land."

"I will have much to tell Adek," Veni said. "But I do not know how it is that you should know so much."

Bapa laughed. "I was a puppet fool around the eating places of Semerang until I found one of your father's workers whose tongue was not sealed with fear. It was he who led me to the house of your schooling on the sixth day, which was yesterday."

"Did you see Sister Patrick?"

"I saw one who was called the Mother, who spoke our tongue and whose word for me was miracle. As your maternal grandmother told me, some of them are good. To me was read the letter that your fingers wrote, and while I heard it and knew where you could come, there was one with an English tongue who wept and another who held her hands in prayer. The one who was called Mother said go at once and, if you can, send a message if you find her, for her eyes hold the blue of the sky for us as they do for you."

"Will you send them a message, Bapa, for Adek and for me?"

"Now I will sleep and the ox rest for the journey to the village where your grandmother waits with anxious eyes. We must make the journey in the silence of night. But the youth who talks to Adek in the early morning light will go with the permission of the respected dalang of this desa."

"Will I write a letter for him to take?"

"No, little bird of Arjuna. The words you wrote have been burned and there will be no others. I will tell the youth the way to go, and he will pass close like a pedlar when the time is right for them to hear his song."

"His song? But what will he sing, Bapa?"

"That the little bird of Arjuna is safe as the blue of the sky."

ABOUT THE AUTHOR

Kathryn Purnell was born in Vancouver, Canada in 1911. She travelled by sea to Australia with her family as a young woman. During the voyage she met and later married Australian scientist William (Bill) Purnell.

Kathryn embodied the soul and spirit of a creative writer. She maintained an intense interest in everything around her, the natural and spiritual worlds, the everyday and the eternal, diverse countries and their cultures, as well as the human condition (of which she had an uncanny understanding). A gifted educator, she was an inspiration to many aspiring writers to whom she taught creative writing. She believed intensely in the need to encourage women writers, the constraints on whom she felt herself at a very personal level.

Bill Purnell's work in the early years of UNESCO as head of its Science Cooperation Division took Kathryn to Paris to live in the immediate post war years, then to Cairo and later Jakarta. She travelled widely in Europe and later spent time in South Africa. Her husband's ill health compelled the family to return permanently to Australia in the late nineteen fifties, It was particularly in this period of her life, with the common pressures of maintaining a family, supporting a husband in his professional life and finding time to create, that she felt most strongly the constraints and limitations placed on the female creative spirit by the societal practices and beliefs of the time. But create she did, both poetry and prose work. She also spent much of her time teaching aspiring writers, mostly women. Active in the Society of Women Writers, in 1998 she won The Alice Award, a biennial award for long-term and distinguished contribution to literature by an Australian woman. Other awards included the State of Victoria Short Story Award and the Moomba Short Story Prize both in 1966/67 and The Society of Women Writers Poetry Prize in 1972. In addition to poetry, Kathryn left a fine legacy of prose writings, much of it unpublished. A current project seeks to redress this by publishing some of her novellas, short stories and her singular novel.

ALSO BY KATHRYN PURNELL

PROSE
The Augustinian Correspondence
Honey Eyes
Apollo in January
Sam in July
In an Urban Forest

POETRY
Safari
Pandora
Harpsichord of Water
Otway Country
Fairy Trees: Poems for the Fitzroy Gardens
The King Walks in the Orangerie

www.ingramcontent.com/pod-product-compliance
Lightning Source LLC
Chambersburg PA
CBHW070031120726
47909CB00003B/1121